DISCARD

D0064429

DISCARD

Good Boy, Achilles!

Eddie Ellis

WESTBOW
PRESS®
A DIVISION OF THOMAS NELSON
& ZONDERVAN

[Scripture quotations are] from the New Revised Standard Version Bible, copyright © 1989 the Division of Christian Education of the National Council of the Churches of Christ in the United States of America. Used by permission. All rights reserved.

This is a work of fiction. All of the characters, names, incidents, organizations, and dialogue in this novel are either the products of the author's imagination or are used fictitiously.

WestBow Press books may be ordered through booksellers or by contacting:

WestBow Press
A Division of Thomas Nelson & Zondervan
1663 Liberty Drive
Bloomington, IN 47403
www.westbowpress.com
1 (866) 928-1240

ISBN: 978-1-5127-5524-4 (sc)
ISBN: 978-1-5127-5526-8 (hc)
ISBN: 978-1-5127-5525-1 (e)

Library of Congress Control Number: 2016914152

Print information available on the last page.

WestBow Press rev. date: 09/26/2016

For Terri and our boys, for Achilles, and,
of course, for the Wounded One.

1

Kssssssss! The air brakes hissed like a giant tire with a leak as the big, yellow school bus slowed to a stop at the end of the old, dirt driveway. Almost before the doors opened, Jeremy bounded down the steps and onto the pavement. Before the bus driver could say, "Bye Jeremy. Have a nice break," Jeremy was running down the driveway toward his family's farm house. The field between the road and the house was only about as big as a football field, but Jeremy was so eager to get to the house it seemed like it was a hundred miles long. About half way there, he passed J.L., his daddy's helper.

"J.L., J.L.! Are they here yet?" Jeremy called.

J.L. looked up from the fence he was fixing and started to answer, but before he could get the words out, Jeremy was gone.

"You'll find out soon enough, little buddy," J.L. chuckled under his breath.

By the time J.L. could raise his hammer to drive the next nail, Jeremy was at the edge of the yard talking to his daddy, who had just come in from the corn field.

"Daddy! Are they here yet?"

"Well, now," his daddy said, kneeling down and putting his hands on Jeremy's shoulders. "What do you say you and I go find out?"

Jeremy's daddy led him around the house to the back yard, where Jeremy's mama was putting new wire on the chicken pen.

"Go ask your mama if they're here yet," his daddy winked.

"Mama, Mama!" Jeremy shouted, running across the yard to the chicken pen. "Are they here yet? Are they here?"

Jeremy's mama smiled and pointed to the slightly open door of the barn. "Go see for yourself."

As his mama and daddy followed him into the barn, Jeremy saw the family's dog, Ginger, stretched out peacefully on a pile of straw in the corner. Then, as his eyes got used to the dim light, he saw in front of Ginger, almost hidden in the thick straw, five tiny puppies!

"They're here, Daddy! Mama, they're here!" laughed Jeremy.

Jeremy started to run toward Ginger and the puppies but stopped when he felt his daddy's strong hand on his shoulder. That hand had kept Jeremy out of trouble before, and he was learning to pay attention to it.

"Hold on, now, Jeremy Dawson," his daddy said. "Remember, those puppies are very small, they're not very strong yet, and they're not really yours. They're Ginger's. She doesn't want you to handle them, and neither do your mama and I. It wouldn't be good for them."

"When will I be able to touch them and play with them?" Jeremy asked.

"When they're a little older and a little stronger," his daddy said. "For now, just look. Don't touch."

The three of them walked over to the pile of straw. Jeremy bent over and put his hands on his knees. The puppies were all lying very still, snuggled close to Ginger. They seemed to be different shades of black and brown, but in the dim light of the barn, Jeremy couldn't tell for sure. The one on the far left stretched its legs, the one in the middle yawned, and the others didn't do anything.

"They're not doing anything," Jeremy said. "They're just laying there."

"*Lying* there, Jeremy," his mother said.

"Lying there," Jeremy repeated. "They don't even have their eyes open."

"Of course," his mother said. "They're just babies—newborns. You didn't do much when you were that age either. But they're beautiful all the same. Five brand-new puppies, all made by the hand of God Himself. You just leave them to Ginger, and they'll be playful little balls of fur in no time. Why, I'll bet one day each of them will be somebody's best friend."

"I guess you're right," Jeremy said. "Just look at them, Mama. Aren't they beautiful?"

"They sure are, Jeremy." Jeremy's mama knelt down and gently stroked Ginger's ear. "Five beautiful puppies—three girls and two boys. Ginger, old girl, you did yourself proud."

2

Jeremy sat cross-legged in the soft dirt between his family's house and his mama's hedge of redtop. His mama had taken good care of that hedge for nearly twelve years, since before Jeremy was born. She was very fond of it, because its red leaves added some color to the yard. Jeremy was fond of it for a different reason. Tall and thick, the hedge surrounded the house, except for the doors, like a leafy moat. The space between the hedge and the house was just big enough for an eight-year-old boy. For Jeremy, that space was another world, a world very different from the one where he spent most of his life. There he dissected flowers and watched armies of ants fight great battles. There he watched caterpillars become butterflies. Now and then, the hedge became the wall of a mighty fortress that Jeremy defended against ship-loads of pirates or armies of trolls. It was *his* place—his secret hideout.

Today, Jeremy wasn't fighting any enemy or watching any wonder of nature. He was just thinking, thinking about the same thing he had thought about every day for weeks now—five things, actually: five little puppies. It had been two weeks since he had come home from school and found them in the barn. Today, like every day this summer, he had gone out to the barn to look at them, and they had done the same thing they always did: nothing—nothing but lie there in the straw with their eyes closed, stretching and yawning. How could anybody sleep so much? Jeremy picked up a clump of dirt, squeezed it, and watched the powdery soil fall through his fingers. The puppies were beautiful all right, but beauty only went so far. Jeremy was ready to run and play with them, to rub their bellies and hear their slurping noises as they licked his ears. Pretty soon, it would be time to give them away, and he wanted to have some fun with them first.

On the other side of the house, the sun was low in the sky. Long shadows hid big slices of the yard like black paint from a bucket kicked onto its side. Eager for a night of prowling, a raccoon poked his head out of a hole in the oak tree on the edge of the pea field. Jeremy heard J.L. slam the door to his old, blue pick-up truck. A stranger would have thought J.L. was angry, but Jeremy knew the latch was so worn that slamming the door was the only way to shut it. As the rumble of the pick-up faded into the distance, Jeremy heard his daddy's footsteps come across the grass from the field to the house. By the time his mama called, "Jeremy, Daddy's home. Go wash up and come help me set the table for supper," Jeremy was already half way to the back door. As the Dawson family sat down at the kitchen table, out in the barn a puppy opened his eyes.

"Well, well," said Ginger, gently nuzzling the little ball of fur next to her. "Hello, Thunder."

"Thunder?" said the puppy. "Am I Thunder? Is that me?"

"Yes. You're the biggest and strongest puppy in the litter. You remind me of a thunderstorm, so I call you Thunder. I thought you'd be the first one to open his eyes and see the world."

"Are you my mother?" Thunder asked.

"Yes," said Ginger. "I am. It's my job to teach you all about the world you live in."

Thunder looked around. The setting sun threw enough light through the slightly open door and the window beside it to let him see most of the barn. In the far corner, two shovels, a rake, and a pitchfork leaned against the walls. To his left, three shelves held a hodge-podge of cans, jars, and boxes. To his right, bags of fertilizer were stacked almost to the rafters. Overhead in the rafters lay fence posts, pipes, and other things that weren't needed for the time being but might come in handy one day. On the floor sat a big tractor, a wheel barrow, a flatbed trailer, and a lawn mower. Thunder didn't know what any of these things were, but some of them looked like awfully fun things to chew on, drag around, hide under, or tear open.

"You have a big job, Mother," he said. "There's a lot in the world, and it looks like fun!"

Ginger chuckled warmly. "Well, this is only the barn. Outside is a big, beautiful world. I'll teach you everything I know about it and about being a good dog."

"Me too? Will you teach me too?"

Startled, Thunder spun around to see who had asked the question.

"Well, what do you know, Thunder?" Ginger said. "One of your sisters has opened her eyes. Hello to *you*, Mist."

"Mist?" asked the tiny, white puppy, moving to Thunder's side.

"Yes, your name is Mist, for the time being."

"For the time being?" asked Thunder.

"Yes," said Ginger. "I'll explain that later, when the others have opened their eyes. Now, I think it's time for you two to meet each other. Mist, this is your brother Thunder."

"Mother calls me Thunder," Thunder roared, "'cause I'm *strong*, like a thunderstorm! What's a thunderstorm, Mother?"

"Well," Ginger answered, "For now, maybe you'd better just remember that, though the storm is strong, the thunder itself is really just noise."

Thunder's ears drooped, and he bowed his head. "Yes, Ma'am."

"Why do you call me Mist?" Mist asked.

"Ginger smiled and nuzzled Mist gently. "I call you Mist because your solid white color reminds me of the mist that sometimes covers the pea field on the Dawsons' farm."

"The Dawsons' farm. That must be part of the world," said Thunder. "See, Mist, this is only the barn. The world's outside. It's big and beautiful. Mother and I will teach you all about it."

"Well, what a nice brother you have, Mist. Tell me, Thunder, just what do you think we should teach Mist first?"

"Well, uh . . . ."

"Hmmf," said Mist. "I think Mother can do just fine without any of your noise, *Thunder.*"

"Oh yeah?" laughed Thunder. With a tiny chirp of a bark, he hopped onto Mist's head and grabbed her ear with his teeth.

Mist rolled onto her back and pushed Thunder's snout upward with both front paws. "Yeah!" Barking, gnawing, and laughing in a way that only puppies can laugh, Thunder and Mist tumbled, stumbled, and chased each other around in the straw, not knowing that already they were learning— learning to run, learning to hop, learning to roll, things all dogs need to know.

As she watched the two puppies play, Ginger rested her head on her front paws and sighed deeply. What would her puppies be like when they grew up? How would their lives be? What troubles would they face? What happiness would they enjoy? When they left her, would they miss her as much as she would miss them? This last thought brought a pain of sadness deep within her, for she loved her puppies with all her heart. Still, she knew that the Father loved all five of them more than she ever could, for His heart was far bigger than hers. She knew He had a special plan for each of them. She would do her job—teach them all she knew—and then tell them goodbye. When they left her, the Father would be with them, and He would be with her. His Spirit would surround them all, and He would fill their hearts with His special peace and joy. Ginger stretched and yawned. The gentle, night air filled the barn as the sun shrank and the shadows grew. Outside, a hoot owl made up a gentle lullaby, while crickets and tree frogs kept time. As the last light faded from the barn, Ginger closed her eyes.

3

Jeremy swallowed his last bit of scrambled egg as he carried his breakfast plate to the sink. The family had just finished eating, and it was his job to wash the dishes. He plugged up the drain, turned on the water, turned the soap bottle upside down, and waited for the tiny bit of soap in the bottom to reach the spout.

"Mama," he called, "We're almost out of soap."

"Hush, Jeremy," boomed the deep voice from the next room.

Jeremy's mama quickly stepped into the kitchen. "Shhh, Jeremy," she said softly. "Daddy's trying to watch the weather report. It's very important. There's a full bottle under the sink. Just get that out if you use up the old bottle."

"They don't know what they're talking about," Jeremy's Daddy muttered as he walked through the kitchen and out the back door, trying to smile.

Out in the barn, the sound of heavy footsteps woke Ginger. She raised her head and looked around. All five puppies lay cuddled close to her, some lying on top of others, still sleeping. Sunlight streamed through the crack in the wall next to her. The space around the door on the other side of the barn was still fairly dark. The sun had just risen. As the footsteps came near the door, Ginger rose to her feet and sniffed the air. When the door opened, she was sitting just inside it, waiting to greet her human. She stretched her neck toward him, with her nose just an inch or so from his hand. He looked down and stroked her head gently. As soon as he touched her, she hopped to his side and pressed her head against his thigh. Dropping to one knee, he took her head in both his hands and began scratching her ears.

"Ginger," he said. "Somehow you always cheer me up. I came out here worried this morning—worried about the weather, worried about my crops, worried about paying bills and sending Jeremy to college. We haven't had much rain lately, and if we don't get some soon, it'll be hard for a farmer to get by. Then you told me good morning, and, somehow things didn't seem quite so bad. You're a good ol' girl, Ginger. I love you."

He held her head against his chest and patted her side. She wriggled free and began to lick his face. "All right," he laughed, turning his face up toward the roof so that Ginger could lick only his neck. "That's enough." He stood up and headed into the barn, as Ginger trotted along beside him, tugging on his pants leg. "That's enough, ol' girl," he said tenderly, climbing onto the tractor. "I'll see you at lunch time." With a roar that nearly shook the barn's walls, he cranked the old tractor and was soon rumbling through the door.

"Wha . . . Wh-what was that, Mother?" came Thunder's voice from behind Ginger as she stood watching the tractor drive away.

"Not 'what,' Thunder, 'who.' That was Evert Dawson, one of my humans."

"One of your . . . *hu-mans?*"

"Yes." Ginger's voice sounded as though it came from the bottom of a deep well filled with love.

"What does that mean, Mother?" asked Mist.

"I'll explain that," said Ginger, turning to face the puppies, "after the others have . . . . Oh, my, what have we here?" Ginger realized that looking back at her were not two but five puppies, all huddled together and trembling in a corner of the barn. The other three had opened their eyes. "Oh, my goodness. Did the noise frighten you, my darlings? There's nothing to be afraid of. Come on out and let me look at you."

All the puppies stayed where they were, until Thunder spoke up. "Come on, everybody. If Mother says it's okay, it's okay."

Thunder trotted out of the corner and sat down in front of Ginger, and the other four puppies followed. "My, my," said Ginger, almost singing the words. "Five beautiful puppies. Ten curious little eyes. Let's see, first things first. Let's get to know each other." She looked at the three who had just opened their eyes. "I believe you've already met your brother Thunder, sort of. He's the biggest one."

"Yeah," said Thunder. "Mother named me Thunder 'cause I'm . . . ."

"Thunder, it's not polite to interrupt."

"Yes, Ma'am."

"Next to Thunder is your sister Mist," Ginger went on. "Thunder and Mist opened their eyes yesterday evening. I'm glad to see the rest of you have joined them. Behind Mist sits your brother Shadow. I call him Shadow because his coat is dark

11

with light specks, like the shadow cast by the Dawsons' peach tree. Beside Shadow is your sister Sunny, whose cheerful face, even before she opened her eyes, reminded me of a sunflower. And the little puppy way in the back I call Wisp, because she is small and gray, like a wisp of the smoke that rises into the sky when Evert burns the fallen leaves in the autumn."

Sunny spoke up. "Evert Dawson. You were going to tell us about him. You said he was one of your humans. What does that mean?"

"Ah, yes," Ginger replied. "My humans. Well, I guess now is as good a time as any for you puppies to start learning about what it means to be a dog in this world. Evert Dawson is a human. That is, human is the kind of creature he is. Just as we are dogs, he is a human."

"Why are humans so noisy?" asked Mist.

Ginger laughed and licked Mist on the nose. "The noise came from the tractor; that's a big tool he uses. He was sitting on top of it. All you need to know about the tractor is that you must stay away from it; it can be very dangerous."

"What do you mean when you say he's *your* human?" asked Wisp.

"By that I mean that the Father has given Evert and me to each other," replied Ginger.

"The Father who created the heavens and the earth?" asked Shadow.

"That's right," smiled Ginger. "But tell me, Shadow, how did you know that?"

Shadow looked at the floor. He crinkled first his left eyebrow and then his right. He cocked his head to the left. Finally, he looked up at Ginger. "I don't know, Mother," he said. "I just knew it, but I don't know how."

"Did the rest of you know it?" asked Ginger.

"Yes, Ma'am," the other four answered, all together.

"How did you know? Can anyone answer that question?" Noses wrinkled. Eyes squinted. Heads cocked. But no one spoke.

"You knew," said Ginger, "because the Father has placed within you a knowledge of Himself."

"You mean we were just born knowing about the Father?" asked Wisp.

"That's exactly right, Wisp," answered Ginger. "Now, as I was saying, the Father has given Evert and me to each other. My mission—the task the Father has given me—is to take care of Evert. I help him; his wife, Audrey; and their son, Jeremy, in any way I can. They're all my humans, and I am their dog."

"Did you help Evert this morning?" asked Sunny.

"A little," Ginger said. "Before the tractor woke you. When he came out to the barn he was very sad and worried, and I cheered him up."

"Why was he worried?" asked Mist.

"I don't know," said Ginger. "I think he may have told me, but, except for a few words and motions, dogs don't understand human language."

"How did you know he was worried?" asked Shadow.

"Even before he reached the barn," Ginger replied, "I could smell his worry. You see, the way humans smell can tell you how they feel inside. When Evert came to the barn this morning, he was very sad and worried. When he spoke, I could hear his worry in his voice, and I could feel it in his skin when he touched me. As he and I greeted each other and played, his smell, his voice, and the feel of his skin slowly changed. By the

13

time he climbed onto the tractor, he was much happier, but still a *little* worried. I think he worries about many things. He always seems sad when the weather is dry."

"Why should he worry about the weather?" asked Wisp. "Doesn't he know that the Father takes care of that?"

Ginger smiled. "He knows, Wisp, but it's still hard for him not to worry. It's hard for many humans. When you pups have your own humans, you may find that helping them with their worries is a big part of your task."

"Our own humans?" asked Thunder. "You mean we're not just going to help you take care of the Dawsons?"

"Oh, no, Thunder," replied Ginger. "You will help me here for a while, but when you are about eight weeks old, you will leave this farm and go to live with other humans. They will be yours, and you will be theirs. You will take care of them, and they will take care of you. They will give you your true names."

"Oh!" exclaimed Mist. "That's what you meant when you said that my name was Mist *for the time being*."

"That's right, Mist," said Ginger. The names I have given to you and the others are only for the time being."

"Tell us more, Mother," said Mist. "You've really only told us a little about how you take care of the Dawsons, and it sounds like a very big job. What will we do for our humans?"

Ginger laughed. "You're right, Mist. It is a very big job. You will care for your humans in many different ways. Sometimes you will cheer them up when they're sad or comfort them when they're afraid. Other times, you will protect them."

Wisp looked around at the other puppies and then looked at herself. Her ears drooped, and her head hung almost to the floor. "How can I protect anyone from anything, Mother? I'm not big enough."

Ginger reached her nose under Wisp's chin and lifted it up. "Sit up straight, Wisp, and listen to me. You will never be as big and strong as your brother Thunder; that is true. But that does not matter. The Father has made you a medium-size dog, and He has a special job just for you. You can do that job better than any other dog. I do not know what the job is, but the Father knows. He has a human who needs *you*."

Wisp held her head high, pricked her ears, and wagged her tail. As Ginger gave Wisp a loving lick on the nose, a tan puppy crept through the early-morning shadows and slipped out of the barn.

Before the last of the soap suds disappeared from the sink, Jeremy had almost finished drying the breakfast dishes he had just washed. His mother often said he could wash and dry dishes faster than anyone she knew, and today he was working *very* fast. J.L. had told him that two weeks ought to be long enough for puppies to open their eyes, and Jeremy was in a hurry to get to the barn. He set his father's coffee mug on the shelf in the cabinet and then turned and reached for the last dish in the drainer: the big platter his mother had used that morning to serve the eggs and bacon. He grasped the platter with his left hand, lifted it out of the drainer, and carefully wiped it dry with the dishtowel. Carefully holding the platter above his head, he placed its end on the shelf where his mother kept it and began to slide it into the cabinet. A few inches from the edge of the shelf, the end of the platter hit a wrinkle in the shelf paper. The platter stopped all of a sudden, but Jeremy's fingers kept moving. He lost his grip, and the platter fell. It hit the counter and then the floor, and pieces of platter flew in all directions. The crash brought Jeremy's mother into the kitchen. She found Jeremy standing beside the counter with the biggest piece of the platter in his hand, and his mouth and eyes wide open.

"Oh, Jeremy!" she cried. She bit her lip, closed her eyes, and walked out of the kitchen. After a long moment, she returned. She knelt on the floor, picked up a piece of the broken platter, and ran a finger softly along its surface. Then she looked up at Jeremy.

She spoke softly and carefully, pausing often. Her voice trembled. "It's all right, Honey. I'll clean this up. I shouldn't have left it for you to put away; it was too big for your little hands. I meant to come take care of it myself, but I got busy and forgot about it. Go out and play. I'll clean it up."

"Mama, I'm so sorry," Jeremy said, his lower lip shaking.

"I said it's okay, Jeremy. Just go outside, *please.*"

"Yes, Ma'am," Jeremy answered. He set the piece of the platter on the counter and looked at his shoes as he walked across the kitchen floor. At the door, he turned to look at his mother. He opened his mouth to speak but forgot his words when he saw her wipe a tear from her face. He turned back to the door and walked out.

Out in the yard, Jeremy picked up a stick from the peach tree and threw it as hard as he could, but it was too light to go very far. It just flipped end over end for a few feet and dropped into the grass. That made Jeremy angry, and he stomped his foot on the ground. He picked up a heavier limb, held it like a baseball bat, and swung it with all his might against the trunk of the tree. It was too green to snap, so it hit the tree with a heavy thud and vibrated, hurting his hands. With a sound that was somewhere between a whimper and a roar, he threw it to the ground and kicked it. Then he kicked the ground. He kicked the ground again and again until he tripped himself and fell.

Worn out, Jeremy struggled to his feet. As his tears started to flow, his shoulders sagged, and he trudged around to the far side of the barn, where his mother would not see him. He fell backwards against the wall and slid his back down it until he was sitting on the ground. He drew his knees close to his chest and rested his forehead on them. He tried to dry his eyes on his bare knees and wished he had worn long pants instead of shorts. The tears felt cold and wet on his skin. Then, he felt something cold and wet on his right ankle. When he lifted his head, he found, sitting in the grass and sniffing at his feet and legs, a little, mostly tan puppy with big feet and floppy ears.

Jeremy wiped his eyes on his shirtsleeves and switched to a cross-legged position. The puppy put his front legs into Jeremy's lap and looked up at him with curious, light-brown eyes. Jeremy put out a hand and scratched the puppy's ear while the puppy licked his wrist. Jeremy looked at the puppy and frowned. He couldn't decide whether to laugh and play with the puppy or go on crying. He had looked forward to this moment for months, ever since he had found out Ginger was going to have puppies. Now that it was here, he was too sad and angry to enjoy it, and that made him even sadder and angrier.

"I'm sorry I'm not in a very good mood right now, pup" Jeremy said in a hoarse voice. "I've had a rough morning. I broke Mama's favorite platter. She told me my great grandma used to serve her cookies on it when she was a little girl. Her mama (that's my grandma) gave it to her when she and my daddy got married. She loved that platter, and I had to go and break it. I didn't mean to; it just slipped out of my hand. She told me it was okay, but I could tell she was sad. When I came outside she was starting to cry."

All of a sudden, Jeremy realized that the puppy had climbed into his lap and that he was now hugging the little dog with both arms.

"Boy, you're an arm full," said Jeremy.

The puppy lifted his head and began to lick Jeremy's face. "Hey, cut it out," Jeremy laughed. The puppy hopped up, rested his front paws on Jeremy's shoulders, and continued to lick. Jeremy fell onto his side, rolled onto all fours, and began to crawl away, but he fell flat on his stomach when the puppy's paws landed on his neck. Then he felt four paws on his back, and his ears were filled with the slurping sounds only a puppy's tongue can make. Jeremy rolled onto his back, grabbed the puppy from beneath, and lifted him into the air. He watched the little red tongue dart in and out of the black and tan snout, missing his nose by inches.

"All right, you little puppy," Jeremy laughed. "I've got you now." He sat up, struggled to his feet, and ran to the back door of the house.

"Mama, Mama," he shouted. "Look what I've got."

"Well, will you look at that?" answered his mother, opening the door. "Isn't that the cutest thing you've ever seen?"

"Look at his feet, Mama," Jeremy laughed. "They're huge!"

"Well, he's just a puppy, Jeremy. He'll grow to them. Of course, he'll have to do an awful lot of growing. My word, he's going to be a whopper! We'll have a hard time finding somebody who wants a dog that big."

Jeremy smiled, and his eyes opened wide. "Really?"

"We'll find a home for him, Jeremy."

19

Jeremy's face fell a bit. "Yes, Ma'am."

"Well, Jeremy, what about the others?" his mother asked. Have you looked at them yet?"

"Oh, yeah!" said Jeremy. He set the puppy on the ground and ran for the barn, with the puppy at his heels and Jeremy's mother following. He ran into the barn and dropped to his hands and knees. When Audrey caught up, she found him awash in a sea of ears and tails. Jeremy screamed his laughter, prompting his mother to cover her ears, as the barking and licking army pursued him around the barn floor. Audrey watched and laughed. There were chores to be done, but after the accident in the kitchen, Jeremy needed a little laughter. Finally, she spoke up.

"All right, Jeremy," she said. "That's enough for now. You have weeds to pull around the hedge. You and the puppies can play some more later."

"Aw, Mama, can't we . . . ."

"Later, Jeremy. Right now, you have work to do."

"Yes, Ma'am."

5

Jeremy followed his mother out of the barn and headed off to do his chores. The puppies followed him to the door, licking his ankles and tugging on his shoelaces. Once he had gone, they went back to playing. They chased each other back and forth, barking, wrestling, and chewing on ears. After a minute or so, Thunder left the group and lay down in the straw beside Ginger.

"Thunder," Ginger asked, "Don't you want to play with your brothers and sisters?"

"I don't really feel like playing any more, Mother," Thunder answered. "Something strange happened to me today. I don't understand it, and I can't stop thinking about it."

"Tell me about it."

"While you were talking to us, I smelled a strange smell coming from outside the barn. It made me want to go outside. No, it made me feel like I *had* to go outside. Outside the barn, I found out the smell was coming from a human, like Evert, only smaller, the same one who came in and played with us a few minutes ago. I figured it was Jeremy, Evert's son. I still didn't really understand what the smell was, but somehow it told me that Jeremy was sad, and that I had to take care of him. I went to him and sniffed him, and he started to scratch my ear, and I could feel sadness in his touch. I liked the scratching; it felt good. As he scratched me, his smell and the feel of his skin changed. Somehow I knew that I was smelling and feeling happiness. It was very faint. It grew stronger for a moment and then faded again. It didn't quite go away, but the sadness was still much stronger."

"That often happens," said Ginger, "in humans, and in dogs. Our feelings can battle within us. We can feel sadness, happiness, and many other feelings all at the same time."

"I don't understand," Thunder said.

"You will," replied Ginger. "For now, just know that the Father understands. That's what really matters."

"As Jeremy scratched my ear," Thunder continued, "he started to make strange noises. I guess he was speaking to me in human language. At first, I could hear sadness in his voice, but then, like his smell and his touch, his voice became happier. I didn't know what he was saying, but I knew that the thing for me to do was to look at him and listen. Then I knew that I should crawl into his lap. He wrapped his arms around me and hugged me. I liked that, too. Then, when he'd stopped speaking, I knew that I should lick his face. When I did that, he made more noises, and his happiness seemed to drive his sadness away. I don't know how, but I understood exactly how Jeremy felt and what I had to do."

Ginger smiled. "And you did well. I was hoping you would when you sneaked out of the barn."

"Oh, you saw me."

"Yes," said Ginger. "I saw you. You see, I smelled the smell too. I knew where you were going, and I knew you wouldn't go far. That's why I didn't stop you."

Thunder lay in the straw for a few minutes, watching the other puppies and thinking. He thought of the smell that had drawn him out of the barn. He remembered the way it had seemed to fill both his body and his mind, telling him what he must do. He had been listening carefully to what Ginger was saying, but when the smell reached his nose, he had completely lost interest. Without thinking about it or knowing why, he had left his brothers and sisters and .... *Left* his brothers and sisters! Thunder lifted his head and looked at his mother.

"Mother," he said. "If I could smell it, and you could smell it, couldn't the others smell it?"

"I'm sure they could," Ginger answered.

"Then why didn't they feel the need to go to Jeremy?"

"That's a good question," Ginger said thoughtfully. "It can only be because Jeremy's smell calls more strongly to you than to your brothers and sisters."

"More strongly," Thunder almost whispered, trying to understand. "Why?"

Ginger smiled the sort of smile that comes only with years of wisdom. "I cannot be sure, Thunder. The ...."

"The Father knows," Thunder interrupted.

"Yes," replied Ginger. "The Father knows."

6

The puppies spent the rest of the morning playing and exploring the barn—rolling in the straw, climbing over bags of chicken feed, chasing each other under the flat-bed trailer, and tearing up worn-out burlap sacks. When they grew tired around the middle of the day, Ginger called them together.

"Now that you've had a full morning of play," she said, "it's time for you to learn about one of the most important parts of being a dog: napping under a tree in the heat of the day."

"Is napping fun?" asked Sunny.

"Fun?" replied Ginger. "Why, it's one of the greatest joys of a dog's life. Follow me."

Ginger led the puppies out of the barn and into the shade of the old oak tree at the edge of the yard.

"What do we do now, Mother?" asked Wisp.

"Now," Ginger answered, settling into the thick, cool grass, "we lie down and go to sleep."

"Mother," Wisp asked, "before we go to sleep, will you explain something to me?"

"Of course," Ginger replied. "What do you want to know, Wisp?"

Wisp cocked her head to the right and wrinkled her brow. "You told us that many humans worry a lot. I still don't understand *why*," she said. "Why can't they just stop worrying and leave everything to the Father?"

"That's a good question, Wisp," Ginger began. "You see, humans are the most wonderful creatures in the world. The Father created this beautiful world with all its animals, and, finally, He created humans. He made the humans very much like Himself, and He told them to take good care of the earth. But then something terrible happened. The humans disobeyed the Father."

The puppies all gasped as they tried to understand. "They disobeyed the Father?" said Thunder. "That's so terrible I can hardly stand to think about it. Why would they do that? Everything the Father tells us is for our own good."

"You're not the first animal to ask that question, Thunder," replied Ginger. "So far, no animal has been able to answer it. I don't know why they did it, but I know they did. And because of what they did, they are less wonderful than the Father made them to be, and the world is filled with suffering and trouble. Things can go wrong in the world; bad things can happen, to humans and to animals. Humans find life in the world very hard. They make bad choices and do foolish things. Though they may try very hard to do what is right, they often do what is wrong. Often their lives are filled with fear, confusion, and sadness. They hurt each other, they hurt themselves, and they hurt the earth. Many of them do not even know about the Father. Some have heard of Him but do not care about Him. Even for those like Evert, who love the Father and try to obey Him, trusting the Father can be hard. So, they make themselves very sad with worry."

"Humans don't sound so wonderful to me," said Shadow. "Why doesn't the Father just do away with all of them?"

"That's the amazing thing," Ginger smiled. "Even though they are not what He made them to be, the Father still loves humans dearly and sees them as the most wonderful creatures in His creation. That's why He's given us dogs the task—the privilege—of taking care of them."

"Privilege?" asked Shadow.

Ginger smiled softly. "Oh, yes, Shadow. A privilege. I love the Dawsons very much, and I am very thankful to the Father for letting me be their dog."

"Love them?" asked Mist. "As much as you love us?"

"Yes," answered Ginger, "but in a different way. Sometimes I feel almost like I'm their mother; other times I feel like I'm their child. They take care of me almost as much as I take care of them. They give me food and shelter, and they help me stay healthy. Even though I know about their weaknesses and their struggles, I look up to them and love them, and I do my best to obey them. After all, they *are* the most wonderful of all the Father's creatures, made in His image. It's kind of hard to explain just how I feel about them, but you'll understand when you have humans of your own."

Ginger stretched and yawned. "Now," she said, "let's take that nap."

"Aww, Mother," Thunder argued, "I don't want to sleep; I want to play."

Shadow and Mist joined Thunder: "Me, too, Mother." The other puppies nodded their agreement.

"That's only because you haven't yet learned how good it feels to nap under a tree on a hot day," Ginger replied. "Just lie down and close your eyes, and you'll see."

As the puppies settled into the cool grass, Sunny raised her head.

"Mother, I have a question, and I don't think I'll be able to go to sleep if I don't ask it."

"Very well, Sunny," Ginger laughed gently. "What is your question?"

"You told us this morning that we would protect our humans. Protect them from what?"

"Other humans, their own bad choices, accidents . . ." Ginger sighed. "You ask many questions, my puppies. I can't answer all of them, because every human life is different, and every day is full of new challenges for a dog. Trust the Father, and believe me: when your humans need your help, you will know what to do."

"How will we know?" asked Sunny.

"Very often your instinct will tell you," said Ginger.

"Instinct?" interrupted Shadow. "What's instinct?"

"Instinct is special knowledge that the Father has given you. At times, you will simply know certain things. You will not know how you know these things, but you will know them as surely as you know that you are a dog. That is instinct."

"Like the way we know about the Father?" asked Wisp. "And the way you know what Evert's smells mean?"

"And the way I knew what Jeremy's smells meant?" asked Thunder.

"Exactly," replied Ginger. "But remember, taking care of humans can be tricky. There will be times when your instinct will not help you. In those times, the Father will make sure you know what to do."

"How will He do that?" asked Shadow.

Ginger smiled a wise smile. "He has His ways. Now, it's nap time."

Ginger and the puppies had just closed their eyes when Mist rose to her feet. "Wait a minute, Thunder. You knew what Jeremy's smells meant? What are you talking about?"

Ginger didn't open her eyes. "Let's not worry about that now, Mist. Lie down and close your eyes."

Mist obeyed her mother, and, after a few minutes, the puppies found out that Ginger was right about napping. They stretched, rolled in the grass to scratch their backs, and yawned, and soon all were fast asleep—all except Thunder. He looked carefully at Ginger to make sure her eyes were closed. Then he stood up and crept toward the house, hoping to find Jeremy.

"Lie down, Thunder," Ginger said, her eyes still tightly closed.

Thunder stopped. "How did you . . . ?"

"Instinct, Thunder," Ginger interrupted. "I like a good nap as much as any dog, but I'm also a mother."

Thunder sighed. "Yes, Mother." He lay down in the grass and stretched. After a few minutes, his eyes began to close, and soon even he was fast asleep. A few hours later, he opened his eyes and saw that Ginger was sitting up and sniffing the breeze. Thunder rose and walked toward her.

"What's happening, Mother?" he asked. The air feels strange, almost like it has thorns in it.

"Don't worry, Thunder," Ginger answered. "Everything's all right. This is the work of the Father, and it's going to make Evert very happy."

By now, the other puppies were awake, huddled close to their mother. The oak tree began to sway, and its leaves rustled as the wind grew stronger. All of a sudden, the whole world seemed to glow very brightly for an instant, and the air itself seemed to roar with anger. The puppies trembled and pressed their heads against Ginger.

"What was that sound, Mother?" asked Thunder.

Ginger chuckled warmly. "*That*, Thunder, was thunder, and *this* is a thunderstorm. We'd better go into the barn."

As the Father's life-giving rain began to wet Evert's thirsty crops, the puppies followed their mother into the barn, where the gentle patter of raindrops on the roof taught them about the joy of napping during a storm.

The sound of a car engine woke Thunder. He didn't recognize it. He often heard cars drive by on the highway, but this one had turned and was coming up the dirt driveway between the pea field and the corn field. Thunder looked around him. He lifted his nose and sniffed the air. Everything seemed to be all right. The sun was almost directly overhead; he had been enjoying a nice nap in the heat of the day. He stood up, stepped out from under the tea olive bush, shook from head to toe, and stretched. He and the other puppies were six weeks old now and allowed to roam free on the Dawsons' little farm.

Thunder watched as the car approached. As it pulled into the yard, he backed into the safety of the tea olive. Ginger had taught him and the others to stay away from moving cars. When the car stopped and its engine fell silent, Thunder joined the other puppies in running to greet it. Before they reached the car, a rear door swung open, and out hopped a small girl about Jeremy's size. Without closing the door, she ran toward the puppies and fell to her knees, welcoming the wagging tails and darting tongues. Since the car had come to a stop near the tea olive, Thunder reached her first, but no sooner had he arrived than Wisp leaped over him, nearly knocking him down, and began to lick the little girl's face.

The sound of the screen door caught Thunder's attention, and he turned to see Jeremy run out of the house followed by Audrey. The girl stood, and she and her mother traded greetings with Audrey and Jeremy. Thunder could tell by their behavior and their smells that they were friends. Then the girl turned and began to walk among the puppies as they hopped, pawed, and tugged. She picked up Mist, stroked her for a moment, and set her back down. She stooped and scratched Sunny's ears. Shadow grabbed her pants leg from behind, and she knelt to keep from falling as the puppy tugged playfully.

Thunder was just about to run to the girl and lick her face when he suddenly found himself in the dark. When he tried to run, he found that his path was blocked on four sides and from above. He began to whine and then to yelp. Suddenly, the light returned, and he saw Jeremy holding a box and listening to his mother. Neither Jeremy nor his mother smelled or sounded happy.

Eager for his chance to meet the visitor, Thunder trotted to the little girl and licked her sandaled foot. She bent over and patted his head. She stood and looked for a few minutes and finally scooped up Wisp and carried her to her mother. The tall, thin woman stroked Wisp's head and pinched her daughter's nose. The little girl set Wisp down, and after speaking briefly with Audrey and Jeremy the two climbed into the car and drove away as the puppies scattered. Speaking harshly, Audrey led Jeremy into the house.

"Mother," said Mist, "What just happened?"

Ginger looked both happy and sad. "Unless I miss my guess," she said pleasantly, "Wisp was just chosen."

"Chosen?" asked Wisp.

"Chosen," Ginger answered. "That little girl is Jeremy's cousin Jess. She has chosen you. She and her family will be your humans. In a couple of weeks, they will come back to get you."

"I like her," said Wisp. "I liked her before I even saw her— the second I smelled her."

8

"Sit down on that couch, young man," ordered Audrey. Jeremy sat.

"Exactly what were you trying to pull—putting that box over that poor, little puppy?" his mother demanded.

"I just didn't want her to pick him," Jeremy said. "For all I care, she can have all the others; I just don't want anybody to take Achilles."

"Well, you listen to me . . .," Audrey stopped. Her voice grew softer. "Achilles? You've named them?"

"Not all of them. Just Achilles. He's my favorite."

"Why would you name him Achilles?"

"We read a story about Achilles in school," Jeremy half mumbled, half moaned. "He was a great warrior. I thought any dog as big and strong and pretty as him deserved a name like Achilles."

Audrey sat down next to Jeremy. She brushed the hair from his forehead and pulled him close to her. "Son, I know you love that puppy. I watch you play with him every day. But, the fact is, we can only afford to take care of one dog, and that's Ginger. We'll make sure all the puppies get good, loving homes, but we can't keep any of them."

Jeremy looked up. "But you said we might not be able to find anybody to take a dog as big as Achilles. And if we can't find anybody . . . ."

"I said it would be hard, and I was really just kidding. We'll find someone. Understand?"

"Yes, Ma'am."

"Okay, honey. You can go now. Walk, and don't slam any doors."

Jeremy stood up and walked into his bedroom, shutting the door quietly behind him. Audrey looked out the window at Thunder. He was truly a fine puppy. At six weeks, he already weighed about twenty-five pounds. His big feet, thick legs, and strong shoulders promised that he would grow to be a very powerful animal. She had seen him get the better of Jeremy in tug-o-war several times. His coat was mostly tan, deepening almost to a reddish shade along his back. His ears and snout were black with tan flecks. The ears did not stand up straight but pricked in a handsome way when a sound caught his attention. His light brown eyes were surrounded by what looked like black shadows—not rings, shadows. From the outer corner of each eye a thin black stripe curved downward an inch or two and grew at its end to a small black spot the shape of a teardrop. His belly and chest were white, and just below his throat the white area split into three branches that looked a little like the head and wings of an angel. His cheeks, like a wolf's cheeks, sported thick tufts of hair. His thick, wolf-like tail was mostly tan and sprinkled with black. He was simply beautiful, one of the most beautiful puppies Audrey had ever seen. Jeremy had named him well. He surely knew how to pick a dog, but facts were facts. The family just couldn't afford the food and vet bills for another dog.

Jeremy fell face first onto his bed and buried his head in his pillow. He lay there, still and silent, until his neck began to hurt. Then he rolled onto his back and stared at the spot on the ceiling where his daddy had patched a leak years before. He shed no tears. He didn't smile; he didn't frown. He was too wrapped up in his feelings to show them on the outside. He just lay there, his face as still as a statue's.

He knew the puppies had to go. He had known it all along. He had known he shouldn't grow to love any of them, but he couldn't help it. Thunder was fast becoming his best friend—always glad to see him, always full of love, always ready to listen to anything Jeremy wanted to say. Jeremy loved the puppy with a love that he thought must be kind of like the love his parents had for him, the love he would one day have for his own children. One day soon, someone would come and take his best friend away.

Around three o'clock, Audrey came into the room and brought Jeremy some fresh-baked chocolate chip cookies—his favorite—and a glass of milk. Jeremy didn't speak or move. He just stared at the spot on the ceiling.

"Jeremy," his mother said softly, "You're being a good boy. As good as I could expect. I know you're very disappointed, but you didn't throw a tantrum. I'm proud of you for that. You need some room to be sad. I'll leave you alone."

Jeremy remained silent and still as his mother stepped out of the room and softly closed the door. When he looked at the clock, it was about five o'clock. He had had as much of his bedroom as he could stand. He rolled onto his feet and, still not speaking, walked out of his room and toward the back door.

Out in the yard, Thunder was playing chase with Mist and Sunny. He was just about to pounce on Mist when he heard the screen door slam shut. He stopped and sniffed.

"You're lucky, Mist," he called over his shoulder as he headed toward Jeremy. "I gotta go."

Thunder knew that smell, and he knew what it meant. It was the same smell that had come from Jeremy the day the two first met, but this time it was much stronger. Jeremy was sad—very sad. Thunder knew what he had to do. Jeremy walked down the back steps and headed around the house toward the corn field. Thunder caught up with him, sat down in his path, and wagged his tail. Without looking down, Jeremy stepped over Thunder, nearly tripping, and kept going. Thunder ran after him, grabbed his shoelace, and tugged so hard he nearly pulled Jeremy down. Jeremy spoke loudly and harshly, and a new smell came from him. Thunder's instinct told him it was the smell of anger. Thunder tucked his tail between his legs, bowed his head, and twisted his neck to look up at Jeremy. He had never made Jeremy angry before, and he was eager for forgiveness. As Jeremy started to run toward the corn field, Thunder barked and chased him. Jeremy stopped, picked up a stick, and threw it at Thunder. The smells of sadness and anger were now stronger than ever. They drew Thunder toward Jeremy, but another stick drove him back, and Jeremy spoke even more loudly and more harshly than before. Suddenly, Jeremy turned and ran faster than Thunder had ever seen him run toward the corn field. Heeding the smells and his instincts, Thunder followed. More than he had ever wanted anything, he wanted to be with Jeremy and to see him through whatever trouble he was facing. Then a hand with strength such as he had never felt caught Thunder under the chest and held him fast.

"Easy, Thunder," said a voice. "Let's talk." The voice was powerful and friendly. It sounded both close and far away. It seemed to come from all around Thunder. With everything that made him a dog, Thunder still wanted to follow Jeremy, but somehow he knew he must obey the voice. Turning around, he looked up to see a man, like Evert, but different. He was bigger than Evert, bigger than any man Thunder had ever seen, and he seemed to be filled with light. He didn't create light, like the sun or the Dawsons' porch light, and he didn't reflect light, like the mirrors on the cars Thunder had seen. He looked as though he had been in the presence of pure light and was soaked with it, like a sponge soaked with water. The light made the man stand out from everything around him. Compared to him, the rest of the world looked gray and dim, as though he was all that was real and the rest of the world was just an old, faded picture. Thunder thought he smelled peace and joy coming from the man, but then he realized that the man had no smell. Some other sense that Thunder did not understand told him about the state of the man's mind. Thunder sat quietly before him and waited for him to speak again.

"Thunder," the man said, "Jeremy is very sad and angry right now. Your instincts told you to follow him and comfort him. When you tried, he drove you away, and that has made you sad."

At that, Thunder thought for the first time about how badly Jeremy had hurt his feelings. Until then, he had been too worried about Jeremy to think about himself.

"Don't worry, Thunder," the man continued. "Jeremy has not turned against you; he loves you dearly. Earlier today, his mother told him that you would have to leave, that they could not let you stay here. Because of his great love for you, that broke Jeremy's heart, and he began to wish that he did not love you so much. When you tried to comfort him, he thought of his love for you and of the pain which that love had caused in his heart. He thought that if he stopped being your friend, the pain would go away. He is in the corn field now, crying. Soon, he will figure out that turning his back on you will not make him feel better, and he will regret what he did to you. Then he will come back, and you will have the chance to comfort him. Until then, wait."

"Why can't I stay with Jeremy?" asked Thunder. "Where will I go?"

"I do not know about that," replied the man. "The Father knows."

"You know about the Father?" asked Thunder.

The man chuckled. "Oh, yes. I know about the Father."

Thunder closed his eyes as he thought about all that the man had said. When he opened them, the man was gone. Thunder looked around him and blinked a few times. Now that the man had left with the light he carried, Thunder's eyes had to adjust. After what he had seen, he was so amazed that he felt dizzy. He staggered into the shade of the peach tree and lay down beside Ginger. He lay there for a long time before either of them spoke.

"You look confused, Thunder," Ginger said. "In fact, you almost look lost. What is it?"

"It's hard to explain, Mother," Thunder began. "A little while ago, Jeremy came out of the house sad and angry. I tried to cheer him up, but he ignored me and headed for the corn field. When I followed, he threw sticks at me and ran. I started to chase him, but a man stopped me."

"What man?" asked Ginger.

"I don't know. He was very strong, and . . . light . . . bright light. . . ."

Ginger raised her head from her forepaws. "Thunder, you have had a visit from one of the shining messengers."

"Shining messengers?" asked Thunder. "You know about these messengers?"

"I have seen a few of them in my life, not many. They come from the Father. They do His work and carry His words."

"Words," said Thunder, lifting his head. "*Yes.* He spoke to me, and I understood his *words.*"

"Of course you did," Ginger replied. "He spoke the words of the Father. Those words you will *always* understand."

Thunder told Ginger all that the shining messenger had told him—that he would have the chance to comfort Jeremy soon.

"Maybe sooner than you think, Thunder," said Ginger, looking toward the corn field. Thunder turned toward the field and saw Jeremy walking slowly into the yard. Thunder stood up and trotted toward him and then stopped a few feet away from him. He approached Jeremy slowly, with his head held low. Jeremy fell to his knees and wrapped his arms around Thunder. Thunder smelled and felt his sadness and, mixed with it, a great feeling of love. He pressed close to Jeremy and licked his face. Jeremy spoke many words that

Thunder could not understand. But in the midst of them, Thunder heard several times one word he had learned to recognize, a word Jeremy said to him often: Achilles. Thunder thought that must be Jeremy's name for him.

After a few minutes, they heard the familiar sound of Evert's tractor returning from the field. Jeremy gave Thunder one last squeeze, stroked his head, and went into the house. By now the sun was low in the sky, and the yard was streaked with shadows. In the dim light Thunder saw Evert Dawson walk across the yard and disappear through the back door of the house.

Thunder lay in the yard for a long while staring at the lighted windows of the house, thinking of his great love for Jeremy, and wondering why he had to leave and where he would go. Then he remembered the words of the shining messenger. "The Father knows," he said to himself, and he felt peace. There was much he didn't understand, but he trusted the Father. After a long while, the windows became dark, one by one, and Thunder made his way back to the barn to join Ginger and the other puppies. Just as Thunder was drifting off to sleep, a deep growl from his mother woke him and the others.

9

Ginger was on her feet, and the hair on her back was standing up. All the puppies sniffed the air.

"That's a scary smell, Mother," said Sunny. "What is it?"

"Stay here—all of you," said Ginger. Snarling, Ginger moved gracefully through the barn door and into the night. After a few seconds, the puppies heard their mother's barking and growling, the slamming of a door, shouting, and heavy footsteps. Then they heard Evert Dawson's voice speaking calmly and gently. Soon Ginger came back into the barn.

"What happened, Mother?" the puppies asked, almost in one voice.

Ginger lay down in the straw and began to nuzzle her puppies one by one. "There was a bad man here," she said. "A burglar. I chased him away. Everything's all right. Settle down, and go to sleep."

"Way to go, Mother!" said Thunder.

"It wasn't fun, Thunder. Being a watchdog is not a game," Ginger said. "I only did what I had to do to protect my humans."

"I see, Mother," said Thunder.

"Mother," Mist said. "If this man was bad, he might have hurt you. You might have even been . . . ."

"Killed," Ginger replied. "That is true, Mist. Sometimes, that's a dog's task. I am willing to give up my life to protect my humans."

"That's a lot to give," Sunny said.

"Yes," answered Ginger. "But not *too* much. The Wounded One did not think it was too much. If it was not too much for him, it is not too much for us."

"The Wounded One?" asked Shadow. "Who is the Wounded One?"

"I can tell you only that he is the Son of the Father, and yet he and the Father are one. He is wonderful and glorious, and the Father has given him all power. Many years ago, the Father sent him into the world. He gave up his life and then returned from death to give life to the humans."

"I don't understand," remarked Sunny.

"Neither do I," Ginger answered. "It is something too big for the minds of dogs, even for the minds of humans."

"Does the Wounded One ever visit dogs?" asked Thunder. "Like the shining messenger visited me?"

"I have heard that he does at times," said Ginger. "I have never seen him. I know only that, if you see him, you will know him by the scars on his wrists and feet and in his side."

The puppies fell silent, trying to understand what Ginger had told them about the Wounded One, but it was too big for their minds. They thought and thought until their eyes grew very heavy, and, one by one, they gave in to sleep.

10

As Jeremy helped his mama wash the breakfast dishes, he looked out the window and saw J.L.'s old blue pick-up coming up the driveway. In the east, the sun painted the sky red as it peeked above the horizon. Already, the late-July air was warm, but a gentle breeze brought a mild beginning to what was sure to be a hot day. In the treetops, the birds sounded the first notes of morning, announcing that they were ready to go to work and the crickets could take a rest. Delighted with the new day, the squirrels chased each other up and down the trunks, their tiny claws clicking and scratching a wake-up call against the bark.

"What time do you think they'll get here, Mama?" Jeremy asked as he dried Evert's favorite coffee mug.

"Pretty early, I expect," answered Audrey. "Jess is mighty excited about getting a puppy. I talked to Miriam on the phone yesterday evening, and she told me Jess had been marking off the days on her calendar. I bet she hardly slept last night."

Jeremy laughed. He had always liked his cousin Jess. He had only a few relatives who were his age, and Jess was the only one who lived nearby. The two always had fun when they were together. They had passed many an afternoon together on their grandma's porch, Jeremy's toy army men guarding Jess's dolls against the evil monsters that prowled the yard. Now that they were older and were allowed to walk to the creek that ran next to their families' farms, they often fished together on the soft, shady bank. If Jess hadn't been Jeremy's cousin, she still would have been his good friend. So today Jeremy was eager to see Jess and very happy to give her a puppy, especially since she had already picked one, and it wasn't Thunder.

"Mama," Jeremy asked. "How long do you think it will take to find homes for the other four puppies?"

"Probably not very long," Audrey answered. "Your daddy put up signs yesterday at the post office and the grocery store. Everybody in Pondberry goes to those two places, so it ought not to take long to find four people who are interested in free puppies. Now, I have some book-keeping to do. When you've finished up here, why don't you go outside and wait for Jess?"

While Jeremy dried the last dish from breakfast, Audrey went into the little room she and Evert used as an office. After he'd put the dish into the cabinet, Jeremy hung up the dish towel and went outside. He found Ginger in the shade of the peach tree, sat down next to her, and began stroking her ear.

"Good morning, girl," said Jeremy. "Today's the day, huh?" Ginger turned toward him and licked his nose. All of a sudden, the two paws on top of his head told Jeremy that his best friend had found him. Jeremy covered his head and laughed as the paws slid down to his shoulders. Reaching behind him with one arm, he pulled the tan ball of fur around him and into his lap.

"Hi there, Achilles," Jeremy said. "Today's a big day. My cousin Jess is coming to get your sister. She's going to be Jess's dog now. How 'bout that? Huh?" Jeremy rolled onto his knees, grabbed the little dog's head in both hands, and made a playful growling noise. Thunder barked a playful bark, picked up a small stick, ran a few steps, and then turned to look at Jeremy. Jeremy rose to his feet and was about to give chase when he heard the sound of a car coming toward the house on the dirt driveway.

"Mama," he called. "They're here!"

When his mother opened the door, Jeremy ran to the edge of the yard and waited. After a moment, his mother appeared beside him.

"That's not Miriam's car," Audrey said. "I wonder who it is."

The two watched as a small, green car slowed to a stop at the end of the driveway. The door opened, and out stepped a young man who looked to be around 25 years old.

"Good morning," the man said.

"Good morning," came the reply.

"I'm guessing you're Mrs. Dawson," the man said, looking at Audrey.

"Yes, Audrey Dawson," Audrey answered. "And this is my son, Jeremy."

"Hi, Jeremy," the man said.

"Hi," came Jeremy's reply.

The man looked at the puppies, who were now crowded around his feet, and smiled. For a few seconds he said nothing. He seemed to have forgotten that Jeremy and Audrey were there. Then he looked up again, with a big smile. "My name's

45

Don Hewitt. I'm new in the area," he said. "Just moved into a little house in Pondberry. I live alone. I was just thinking yesterday that it would be nice to have a dog to keep me company. Then I saw your sign at the grocery store, so I thought I'd come out and take a look at your puppies."

"Well, welcome," said Audrey. "Here they are. They've had all their shots, and they all need homes, except for the smallest one. She's already spoken for."

"I can see why. She's a real beauty, but then so are all the others."

"Well, look them over, and, if you want, take your pick."

Mr. Hewitt knelt down and scratched Thunder's ear. "Boy, aren't you something!"

Jeremy started toward Thunder but stopped when he felt his mother's hand on his shoulder. Thunder wagged his tail and licked Mr. Hewitt's hand. "Friendly, too, huh?" Mr. Hewitt said. "I had a dog a lot like you when I was about Jeremy's age. I sure miss that dog."

"You can't have that one," Jeremy shouted. "He's my favorite."

Mr. Hewitt looked up at Jeremy and then at Audrey.

"Jeremy!" Audrey's voice sounded a little shaky. "If Mr. Hewitt wants that puppy, he can have him. We've already talked about this. If you can't be polite, you're going to have to go to your room."

Mr. Hewitt smiled and then looked at Thunder again. "But you're going to be a very big dog," he said, "and my yard's a little too small. I don't think you'd be happy there."

"Really, Mr. Hewitt," said Audrey. "If you want that one, you can have him."

"Mama," whined Jeremy. "He said his yard was too small. Don't . . . ."

"Jeremy!" Audrey interrupted, sounding a bit firmer. "Go to your room. Now."

"Yes, Ma'am," Jeremy mumbled, walking toward the house.

Suddenly, Mr. Hewitt laughed loudly at the slurping sound in his right ear. "Well, what have we here?" he asked, turning to stroke Mist's back. "Hey, you're a cute little thing. Would you like to come home with me?" Mist wagged her tail and licked Mr. Hewitt's out-stretched hand. He lifted her to his chest and stood up, cradling her in his arms and gently scratching her ears.

As Jeremy stepped into the house, Audrey's eyes turned back to Mr. Hewitt. "As I was saying, if you want the tan one, you can have him. Jeremy knows we're not going to keep him, and I'm afraid the longer the puppy stays, the harder it'll be for Jeremy when we finally give him away."

Mr. Hewitt smiled. "Thank you, Ma'am. I'm sure you're right, but my yard really is too small for a big dog. I think this little white one will grow up to be just about the right size. She'll be pretty big herself, but not huge like her brother there."

"All right, then," said Audrey. "She's yours, and I can tell you'll take very good care of her."

"That I will, Mrs. Dawson. She and I will be best friends, and I always look out for my friends."

"That's good to hear," Audrey smiled. "Now, if you'll wait here, I'll get you her vet records."

Mr. Hewitt set Mist on the ground and waited. Ginger called her puppies together. "Well, my darlings," she said. "It looks like the time has come. You are old enough to leave now, and that man has chosen Mist. When Audrey comes back, he will leave and take Mist with him. Sometime today, Jess probably will come for Wisp. Before long, all of you will have left. You will go to your new homes to take care of the humans the Father has given you. I have taught you all that I can. Anything more that you need to know the Father will teach you in His own way. Your leaving will be sad for all of us, but the Father will always be with us. His Spirit will surround us with His love and fill our hearts with the joy that only He can give."

Ginger gave Mist a loving lick on the nose. The other puppies surrounded Mist, licking, nuzzling, and barking their goodbyes. By now, Audrey had returned. Mr. Hewitt reached down and scooped Mist into his arms. Mist climbed up his chest and licked his face.

"All right, girl," Mr. Hewitt laughed. "Let's go home."

Audrey held out the envelope with Mist's records. "Here you are, Mr. Hewitt. Our phone number is with the records. If you have any questions, feel free to call."

"Thank you, Mrs. Dawson," he said, taking the envelope. "And thank you for the puppy. You have a good day."

Jeremy watched from his bedroom window as Mr. Hewitt climbed into his car with Mist and headed up the driveway. Long after the car had gone out of sight, Jeremy stood with his forehead pressed against the glass, thinking about how much the world seemed to have changed all of a sudden. The swaying of the branches in the peach tree told him that the gentle breeze was growing into a fairly stiff wind. Today would be a good day to fly his kite over the pea field, but Jeremy didn't care.

Backing away from the window, he found the edge of his bed and flopped backward onto the mattress. He looked over to the wall at the chart he was using to keep track of his progress in his school's summer reading program. One more book, and he'd have a coupon for a free pizza, but Jeremy didn't care.

He rolled onto his side and saw his fishing pole leaning in the corner. This would be a good morning to take some bread dough or worms down to the creek and catch bluegills, but Jeremy didn't care. The things that would have seemed fun the day before didn't seem to matter now.

Everything seemed different, because now Jeremy knew, really knew, that the puppy he loved, almost as much as he loved his mama and daddy, was going to leave, and probably soon. Of course, he had known all along that one day he would have to tell the puppy goodbye, but up to now that day had seemed far away, almost not real. Now, he knew that the next car that came up the driveway might leave with his best friend. Jeremy was so lost in his thoughts that he didn't hear the car doors shut out at the edge of the yard.

"Jeremy," Jeremy heard his mama call. "Miriam and Jess are here. Come on out and say hello to them." Jeremy took a deep breath and let it out in a long sigh. He rolled off his bed and onto his feet and headed for the front door.

Out at the edge of the yard, Audrey waited to greet her sister-in-law and niece. The car had barely come to a stop when a rear door flew open and Jess jumped out. After a few steps, she stopped, looked around the yard, and then ran straight for Wisp, who was just coming out from beneath the tea olive bush along with Shadow.

Audrey laughed as the streak of blue dress and blonde curls ran past her. "Good morning, Jess. How are you doing?"

When Jess reached Wisp, she fell to her knees, flopped onto her side, and began to roll around in the soft grass, laughing with glee, as Wisp and Shadow licked her face and tugged at her pigtails.

"Jess," Miriam laughed, "Don't you think you ought to come over here and speak to your Aunt Audrey?"

Jess struggled to her knees and gathered Wisp into her arms. She stood up and walked over to her mother and aunt, hugging the puppy tightly and rubbing her nose against the top of the fuzzy head as she went.

"Good morning, Aunt Audrey," she giggled.

"Good morning, Jess, I see you didn't have any trouble remembering which puppy was yours."

"No, Ma'am," Jess smiled. "This is the one."

"What are you going to call her?" asked Audrey.

"Dumplin'," Jess answered.

"That's a stupid name," came a voice from behind her.

Jess wheeled around. "It is not, Jeremy; it's a cute name. And anyway, she's *my* puppy now, and I can call her anything I want."

Miriam put her hand on Jess's shoulder. "Settle down, Jess. Let's not get in a fight."

"Of course it's a cute name, Jess," Audrey said. "Jeremy's just in a bad mood; he's had a hard morning. Someone almost took his favorite puppy today. But that's no excuse for being mean. He's going to have to be nicer or go to his room." Audrey paused. "Jeremy, I'm waiting."

Jeremy sighed. "I'm sorry, Jess. I didn't mean it. I hope you and Dumplin' have a lot of fun together."

"Well," Miriam said, "I wish we could stay and visit, but I have a lot to do today. We'd better get going. Jess, what do you say?"

"Thank you for the puppy, Aunt Audrey," Jess said, as her whole face seemed to disappear behind a bright smile.

"You're welcome, Sweetie," Audrey replied.

Jess turned toward Jeremy. "Thank you, Jeremy."

Jeremy, who was staring at his shoes, looked up, trying hard not to frown. "You're welcome," he said quietly.

"Okay, honey," said Miriam to Jess. "Let's get going. Bye now."

As the car turned around and headed down the driveway toward the hard road, Jeremy could see Jess's head bobbing up and down with laughter as Dumplin' licked her face. He could see Miriam smiling as she watched her little girl play with her new puppy. Looking up at his mother, he saw laughter in her eyes. Everyone was happy—everyone but Jeremy. He wanted to be happy; he had looked forward to giving Jess one of the puppies. But he couldn't be happy. He was about to lose his best friend. Didn't they know that? Didn't they understand how terrible that was? Didn't they care? Everybody else just went right on being happy, and Jeremy was stuck in his sadness. It didn't seem fair, and Jeremy felt all alone. Then he felt a familiar touch. When he looked down, he saw his best friend's head pressed against his leg. He sat down in the grass, and Thunder curled up in his lap. As Jeremy scratched Thunder's ears, the puppy stretched and yawned. If there was anything in the world better than having his ears scratched by Jeremy, Thunder didn't know what it was. Jeremy looked down at the puppy and smiled. For a few moments, he forgot his sadness. He felt as though he had floated away to another world, a world where it was always warm enough for swimming and breezy enough for kite flying, where worms were easy to find and the fish were always biting, and where little boys never had to say goodbye to puppies. Of course, he still knew that soon his best friend would have to leave. But that was away in the back of his mind. For the moment, he and Thunder were together, and, in the special world that their friendship created for him, Jeremy was happy. Then his mama's voice pulled Jeremy back into this world.

"Jeremy, don't you have some chores to do this morning?"

"Yes, Ma'am."

As Jeremy headed off to clean the chicken pen, Thunder joined Shadow and Sunny in a game of chase. The three puppies ran here and there, this way and that way around the yard, barking and growling so that a stranger might have thought they were angry at each other. They took turns chasing and being chased—one chasing two, then two chasing one, then one chasing one while the third ran around and barked for joy, chasers becoming runners and runners becoming chasers, all of a sudden and without complaining. They looked a little like leaves blown here and there by the wind. No human really understands the rules of this game, but all dogs know them by instinct. It's one of their favorite games.

As the puppies ran to and fro, Sunny spoke up. "Boy, it sure seems strange playing chase with only three of us instead of five."

Thunder, who had been running from Sunny, quickly turned and began to chase her. "Yeah," he said. "I miss Mist and Wisp already. And Mother and I are going to miss the two of you when you're gone."

Shadow joined the chase. "Wait a minute, Thunder," he said. "How do you know you'll still be here when we're gone? How do you know you won't be chosen before we are?"

Thunder made a sharp turn to run from Sunny, who had begun to chase him and Shadow. "I'm Jeremy's dog. That's how. I'm staying right here on this farm. I'm Jeremy's dog, and Jeremy's my human. And, by the way, my name's Achilles. That's what Jeremy calls me."

Sunny ran past Thunder and headed him off, forcing him to turn again. "You can't be sure about that," she said. "Mother says all of us puppies are leaving the farm."

"I can too be sure."

"Cannot!" Shadow and Sunny answered.

"Can too!"

"Cannot!"

"Can too!"

"Quiet! That's enough!" At the sound of his mother's voice, Thunder realized that he had stopped running and was standing in one place, shouting at his brother and sister. "What is going on here?" Ginger demanded.

"Mother," Shadow said, "Thunder says he's not leaving this farm."

Thunder held his head high and puffed up his chest. "Achilles, not Thunder."

"*Thunder*," Sunny protested, "says he's sure he's going to stay here because he's Jeremy's dog."

Ginger sighed, and her ears drooped a little. "I see. Shadow and Sunny, you two run along and play. Thunder and I need to talk."

As Shadow and Sunny went back to their game of chase, Ginger led Thunder into the shade of the peach tree, and the two of them lay down in the soft, cool grass. For a moment that seemed to Thunder like much more than a moment, Ginger remained silent. Then she spoke. "Thunder, what makes you so sure you're going to stay here on this farm?"

Thunder lowered his head and looked up at his mother timidly, "My name is Achilles, Mother."

"Thunder, what makes you so sure you're going to stay here on this farm?"

"I love Jeremy, and he loves me. I *must* be his dog. We're best friends. I *must* be his dog."

"Maybe you *are* Jeremy's dog. Maybe your true name *will* be Achilles. But for now, we don't know what is going to happen. Only the Father knows. For now, your name is Thunder."

"Yes, Ma'am. My name is Thunder. But just you wait, Mother. You'll see. I'll stay on this farm, and my name *will* be Achilles. I'm Jeremy's dog."

Ginger thought for a moment. "Thunder, the night you opened your eyes, the barn was all you could see. So you thought the barn was the world. Now, even though you know that there is a big world beyond this farm, this farm is all you can see. So it seems to you as though this farm is the whole world. The Father knows the whole world—every human and every dog in it. If the Father wants you to stay here and take care of Jeremy, then you must stay here. But the world is full of humans who need dogs to take care of them, and the Father loves them just as much as He loves Jeremy. If He wants you to leave the farm and take care of one of them, then you must go, and you too will come to love that person as much as you love Jeremy. Remember, the Father has a plan, and His plan is always best, even though it may not always be what seems best to us."

Thunder laid his head on the ground between his forepaws. "Following the Father's plan is not always easy."

Ginger licked Thunder on the nose. "No, it is not always easy, but it is always good."

12

As Jeremy finished cleaning the chicken pen, he heard the tractor rumble to a stop and saw his daddy walk into the house. It was nearly noon, so Jeremy went inside and washed up for lunch. As he dried his hands, he could hear his parents talking in low voices in the kitchen. He could hear only a little of what they were saying, but he was pretty sure they were talking about him and the puppies, the box he had put over Thunder that morning, and the way he had yelled at Mr. Hewitt. He was almost afraid to go into the kitchen, but the smell of chicken and yellow rice gave him the courage to take his seat at the table. After his daddy had given thanks, the family began eating and talking about what they'd done that morning and what they planned to do in the afternoon. Evert told Audrey and Jeremy about the fence he and J.L. had finished fixing just before lunch.

"That fence is good as new, now," Evert said. "I tried to get J.L. to come eat with us, but he told me he was going to go eat fried chicken with that gal who works at the feed store. I think he likes that gal. Fine with me. That way he'll be in a good mood when he comes back this afternoon to help me clear out the ditches. We'll get a lot of work done today. J.L. always works faster when he's happy. Yep, I really think he likes that gal. I think he'd like to marry her. What do you think, Jeremy?"

Jeremy stared at his plate. "I guess so."

Audrey swallowed a bite of chicken and smiled. "That's nice. J.L.'s a good fellow. I'm glad he's met a nice young lady." She winked at Evert. "I guess pretty soon it'll be time for Jeremy to meet a nice girl and get married."

Jeremy stared at his plate.

"Well, we had a busy morning around here," Audrey continued. "I paid all the bills and brought the books up to date. And Jeremy has that chicken pen looking nice and clean. Don't you, Jeremy?"

Jeremy stared at his plate. "I guess so."

Audrey looked at Evert and sighed. Evert used a piece of biscuit to push some rice onto his fork. "All through with the pen, are you, son?"

Jeremy tried to smile. He was still a little worried about what his daddy might have to say. "Yessir."

Audrey slid a bowl in Jeremy's direction. "Don't fill up on just chicken and yellow rice, Jeremy. You need to eat some peas, too." Jeremy didn't really like peas, but he knew he'd better not argue. He was in enough trouble already.

"I'd eat worms if I thought it would help," he thought to himself.

He took the serving spoon and put some of the peas onto his plate. "Yes, Ma'am."

"Well, it's a good thing you got that pen cleaned up this morning," Evert said. "Because I have another job for you this afternoon."

Jeremy felt his lower lip begin to quiver.

"I want you to go out and find some worms."

"Oh, no!" thought Jeremy. "I *am* going to have to eat worms!"

Then Evert continued, "Because when I get in from the fields this afternoon, you and I are going fishing."

13

"Be careful, Jeremy," Audrey said as Jeremy headed out the back door.

Jeremy jumped from the third step to the soft grass. "Worms are easy, Mama. All I have to do is look under things."

Audrey smiled. "Well, watch out for snakes."

Jeremy rolled his eyes and sighed. "I will."

Jeremy knew of several spots on the farm where worms were easy to find. One was in the shady area between the barn and the old oak tree. There, an old piece of plywood had been tossed aside and forgotten. Beneath it, the ground was always moist, cool, and—best of all—wormy. Jeremy flipped the piece of wood over, and right away he saw several worms squirming in the soft dirt. He picked one up, draped it over his finger, and watched it bend and squirm. He liked worms, because they were squirmy and fun to play with, and, unlike scorpions and snakes, they didn't sting or bite. When he noticed that Thunder had trotted up beside him, he held the worm close to the puppy's nose.

"Hi, Achilles. Want to play with the worms?"

Thunder had never seen an earthworm before, and he was very curious. As any dog would, he tried to use as many of his senses as he could to learn about the strange creature. Jeremy laughed as the little dog pricked his ears, pulled his head back, eased forward, and sniffed. When Thunder tried to lick the worm, Jeremy pulled it away.

"Sorry, boy. That's for the fish."

Without trying very hard, Jeremy quickly found more than a dozen worms. Then he put the wood back where it had been and headed for another favorite spot. At the edge of the wooded area between the house and the creek lay an old tire. Jeremy walked toward the tire carefully and hit it a few times with a long stick to chase out any snake that might be hiding inside. When no snake came out, Jeremy turned the tire over and found ten more worms. Then he looked around in the tall grass and caught five crickets. That would be enough bait for a fun evening of fishing. At least, Jeremy hoped it would be fun.

Most of the time, when Jeremy's daddy said, "Let's go fishing," it just meant he wanted to relax and have a good time fishing with his son. But sometimes it meant he wanted to have a serious talk about something very important. Jeremy didn't really understand why, but serious talks with his daddy were often hard and not much fun. When little boys have serious talks with their daddies, they learn things, sometimes things they don't really want to learn. They learn about facing up to parts of life that are sad or hard. They learn about doing the right thing even when it's not easy. Learning these things is a hard part of the path to manhood, a part that little boys don't always like to walk. So, today, Jeremy was a little scared when he heard J.L.'s truck rumble into the distance and heard his daddy's tractor come to a stop at the barn.

After Evert had washed up a little, he and Jeremy took their fishing poles and the bait and walked down the path from the edge of the yard to the creek. When they came to the water's edge, they sat down in the soft grass. Then they baited their hooks and swung their lines into the water. "Ploink! Ploink!" The two baited hooks hit the water and sank down as far as the corks would let them.

In the west, the sun hung low enough in the sky to cover the creek with the shadows of the tall trees, but it would not set for another hour or so. The late afternoon shadows offered welcome relief from the July heat. As a few leaves floated down the creek, a couple of white, wispy clouds drifted dreamily in the sky, like pieces of a dandelion floating on a gentle breeze. The air was thick with the sounds of birds, frogs, and bugs, so that it seemed almost as if a person could reach out and grab a chirp or a tweet.

Jeremy sat in the grass quietly, staring at his cork, afraid to look up or say anything, wondering whether or not he would enjoy this fishing trip. Evert sat in the grass quietly, watching Jeremy, trying to think of just the right thing to say. Thunder, who had followed the two to the creek, lay quietly in the grass with his head touching Jeremy's leg. He could tell that Jeremy was worried, and he wanted to offer any comfort he could. Evert looked at Thunder and sighed. He loved his boy very much, and he hated for him to be sad. But he knew that sadness was part of life and that, no matter how hard he tried, he couldn't possibly keep sadness away from Jeremy. The best he could do was to help Jeremy learn to face sadness.

Both Jeremy and Evert were so lost in their thoughts that they didn't see their corks go under. Neither one knew he had a fish on his hook until he felt the sharp tug on the line. Suddenly, both spoke at once: "I got one!" Then both raised up their poles and pulled keeper-size bluegills out of the water. As the two fish shook and swung on the ends of the lines, the two lines wrapped around each other so that Jeremy and Evert couldn't tell which fish was whose. Finally, Jeremy managed to grab one of the fish and started to take the hook from its mouth.

"Wait," said Evert. "Let's get the lines untangled first. It'll be easier with the weight of the fish on them. Besides, we want to be able to tell your mama which one you caught."

Carefully, Evert held one fish in his hand and gave the other a shove. Like a tether ball on a rope, the fish swung round and round until its line had unwrapped itself from the other line.

As it turned out, the fish Evert was holding was on Jeremy's line, so Evert handed it to Jeremy and watched as Jeremy quickly took it off the line and placed it on the stringer. Just as Evert was about to grab his fish, the fish gave a hard shake, popped off the line, and hit Evert in the face. As the fish fell, Evert tried to catch it, but he only knocked it toward Jeremy. When Jeremy tried to grab it, he sent it flying into the air and toward the water. In a last effort to save his catch, Evert rushed toward the fish, tripped over a fallen tree limb, and fell face-first into the water. The fish landed on Evert's back, flopped into the water, and was gone.

Soaking wet, Evert pushed himself onto his knees, stood up, and sat down on the bank. He looked at Jeremy, wrinkled his brow, and said, "You're not really a fisherman until you've done something silly like that, son." Slowly, his mouth curved into a frown and his cheeks filled with air. Then, suddenly, he began to laugh like a clown. The two fishermen lay back on the soft grass and, for a few minutes, looked at each other and laughed.

Finally, almost dizzy with laughter, they sat up, baited their hooks, and swung them back into the water. Evert glanced over at Jeremy and noticed that Jeremy was scratching Thunder's ears with one hand and holding his pole with the other, and Evert remembered why they had come to the creek.

"Jeremy, your mama told me you had some trouble this morning. What happened?"

Jeremy spoke quietly and quickly, as though he didn't want to talk but figured he might as well get it over with. "I got mad and hollered at Mr. Hewitt when I thought he was going to take Achilles. Mama sent me to my room. And then I was mean to Jess 'cause I was mad at . . . everybody. Because Achilles has to leave, and I don't want him to."

"You really like that puppy, don't you, son?"

"I love him, Daddy. He's my best friend."

"I know, Jeremy. I wish we could keep him. I really do. But we can't. It costs enough just to take care of Ginger. Keeping that puppy would double our vet bills and more than double what we spend on dog food. That puppy's going to get awfully big, and he'll need a lot of food. That's money we need to spend taking care of you, money we need to put in the bank so one day we can use it to help you go to college."

"I don't need to go to college."

"Yes, you do."

Jeremy stared at his cork for a moment, and then looked up with bright eyes. "I'll pay to take care of Achilles. I'll work and make money."

Evert sighed. He was proud that his son wanted to work hard, but he was sad about the answer that he knew he had to give him. "Jeremy, there aren't too many jobs out there that an eight-year-old can get. Even if you could go around doing odd jobs, we couldn't spare you. We need you here on the farm. You're a big help to your mama and me, and as you grow you'll be a bigger and bigger help." Evert smiled. "Before long, J.L. will be worried that we won't need him anymore."

Jeremy felt tears welling up in his eyes. "Daddy, I don't want to give Achilles away."

Evert blinked and took a deep breath. "I know, son, but we can't always have what we want," he said, as he stroked Jeremy's head. "As you grow, you're going to meet a lot of people and make a lot of good friends. Maybe some of them will be your friends for life, but most of them will be close friends only for a while. Then they'll move on, or you'll move on. Sometimes your mama and I wish we could have you here with us forever, but we can't. One day, you're going to grow up and move away. Oh, we'll still see you, and we'll still love you as much as ever. You'll still be our boy, and we'll still be your mama and daddy. But things won't be the same as when you were living here with us. Part of life is saying goodbye to people . . . and dogs . . . you love. The best you can do is enjoy those you love while they're with you and trust the Good Lord to take good care of them when they leave, or when you leave. I guess the sooner you learn that, the better."

Jeremy looked down at Thunder and stroked his side. The puppy rolled over onto his back, and Jeremy rubbed his belly. "Daddy, is it okay to ask God to take good care of Achilles?"

Evert's voice quivered when he answered. "You bet it is. I think God would like that, and, if Achilles knew, he'd like it too. You want to do that now?"

Jeremy bowed his head and closed his eyes. He thought for a moment. "Lord, if Achilles has to leave here, please give him a good home and people who will be good to him. And help him and me both not to be too sad. . . . But, Lord, if it's okay, please let him stay here. Amen."

Evert chuckled. "Well, I guess I can't blame you for that last part. Now, look here. Something took my bait."

Jeremy pulled his hook out of the water. "Mine too."

Evert and Jeremy stayed at the creek until sundown and caught five more bluegills and a catfish. As they walked home Jeremy thought, for the first time, that, even though serious talks with his daddy were hard, they might somehow be good. When they reached the house Jeremy went inside, and Evert stayed outside to clean the fish. Before he started, he found Ginger, knelt down beside her, and held her head against his chest as he rubbed her ear. "You're a good ol' gal, Ginger. A good ol' gal."

The next day was Sunday, and the Dawsons went to church. In Sunday school, Jeremy's teacher, Mrs. Pemberton, told the children the story of Joseph, who trusted God through many hardships and learned that God would always take care of him wherever he went. Then Mrs. Pemberton asked the children whether they trusted God to take care of them. Jeremy thought to himself, "I hope God will take care of Achilles wherever he goes."

After Sunday school, Jeremy sat with his parents in the morning worship service. Jeremy often had trouble paying attention in the service, and he liked to draw pictures on the bulletin. Monday through Saturday, he drew pictures of airplanes or dinosaurs, but in the Sunday morning church service, he thought it was better to draw scenes from Bible stories. This morning, he drew Joseph in the king's prison. First he drew a bunk. Next he drew Joseph sitting on it, looking sad and lonely. Then he drew a set of heavy iron bars. He was just about to draw a guard when the pencil slipped from his hand and clattered to the hardwood floor. When he bent over to pick it up, the bulletin in his lap bent and crinkled, and Mrs. Terney on the front row turned around to look. Unhappy with the noise, Evert squeezed Jeremy's knee. Jeremy sat up straight and paid attention long enough to hear Preacher Wilkes read John 3:16: "For God so loved the world that he gave his only Son . . . ."

"I know God gave His Son," Jeremy thought, "but do I really have to give up my puppy?"

After the service, all the people went to the fellowship hall for a covered-dish dinner. Most of the women and a few men of the church had spent Saturday evening and part of Sunday morning whipping up their favorite and most famous dishes. Now, in the center of the room stood two long tables placed end to end to form a double-table and covered with platters, bowls, pans, and pots containing all kinds of delicious food. Against one wall stood a smaller table covered with desserts and jugs of water, lemonade, and iced tea—sweetened and unsweetened.

The rest of the room was filled with empty tables lined with empty chairs. The people formed two lines, one on each side of the long double-table. After Preacher Wilkes had given thanks, they began to move along the double-table, from one end to the other, placing food on their plates as they went. Some tried to sample everything but found that their plates weren't big enough for that. Most chose five or six favorites on the first trip to the table and said that they would go back and try other foods a little later, if the other foods were still there.

The empty tables filled up quickly, and some of the men brought in extra chairs so that everyone could sit down and eat. Fried chicken was in huge supply. Most people took some from one platter or another, and, at a few tables, people talked in whispers about whether Stella Bannen or Sarah Nell Carson was the best chicken fryer in the church. Lloyd McClaren's barbecued ribs went fast, and those who planned to get some on the second trip to the table found that they were all gone. Most people enjoyed Ginnie Smithson's potato salad, although some suspected that she had bought it at the grocery store, dumped it into a glass dish, and sprinkled parsley on top of it.

Cora May Bonner's creamed corn, as always, started people asking, "How does she do it?" Some said the secret was to season the corn with bacon, while others said the key was to use real butter instead of margarine. Cora May just smiled and said, "Well, I'm glad y'all like it. I think I did something wrong this time; it doesn't taste right to me." Jeremy heaped his plate with green beans, mashed potatoes, hushpuppies, a drumstick, ribs, and his favorite food in the whole world—his mama's chicken and yellow rice.

Many of the people, after they had finished with the meats, vegetables, and breads, went to the dessert table for Sally Henson's pound cake, Katie Beth Anderson's apple and cherry pies, Louise Williamson's peach cobbler, Martha Pollard's chocolate cake, and several women's chocolate chip cookies. Emma Rollerson always made her cookies from scratch; some other women used store-bought dough. Some folks said they could tell the difference between the made-from-scratch cookies and the others, but they had to admit that all the cookies were delicious. Mrs. Williamson's peach cobbler seemed even better than usual today. Some said it was because this year's peaches were the sweetest in years; others said she must have used more nutmeg than usual. Miss Pollard's chocolate cake, which had won blue ribbons at fifteen county fairs, went fast. The folks who ate it didn't talk about anything; they just ate.

When they had finished eating, Jeremy, Jess, and the other children went out into the church yard to play tag. The adults said things like, "You young'ns be careful," and "Don't mess up your good shoes," and "Watch your little sister," and they went on nibbling on desserts as they chatted about rainfall, the president, and the new quarterback who would be playing in the fall. After an hour or so, they gathered up their platters, their bowls, their jugs, their pans, their pots, and their families and headed home.

When Jeremy's daddy turned the car onto the old, dirt driveway, Jeremy noticed another car turning in behind them. "Why are Mr. and Mrs. Haskin here, Daddy?"

"Mr. Haskin told me today that they were looking for a dog, Jeremy. I told him we had three puppies to give away and invited him and Mrs. Haskin to stop by after church and take a look."

15

Ginger lay in the shade of the peach tree, watching her three remaining puppies play chase. As she watched Thunder, Shadow, and Sunny run here and there, she thought of Wisp and Mist. She wondered what they were doing, how they liked their new homes, and whether they had felt lonely their first night away from the farm. Two puppies were gone now, and the other three probably would leave soon. Saying goodbye to her puppies made Ginger feel a little sad, but deep in her heart she believed that Wisp and Mist were where they ought to be, where the Father wanted them to be. That gave her a feeling of peace. It even made her a little happy. She knew that her peace and happiness were a gift from the Father, she knew that His Spirit was with her and all the puppies, and she was thankful.

Ginger was so lost in her thoughts that she almost didn't notice the sound of the cars coming up the dirt driveway—*almost*, that is. Ginger noticed every sound that came to her ears, and she knew what almost every sound meant. The sound she heard now, the sound of two cars coming up the driveway, told her that the Dawsons were bringing visitors home with them. She thought that just might mean that another puppy was about to leave. The puppies, on the other hand, were still young enough to become so lost in their play that they ignored important sounds. As the puppies played their game of chase, the two cars came nearer to the end of the driveway and the edge of the yard. Ginger was about to bark a warning when Sunny noticed the sound and turned to see the cars coming. "Hey, everybody," she shouted as she ran toward the peach tree and Ginger. "We'd better get out of the way." As the cars pulled into the yard, the other puppies joined Ginger and Sunny under the tree. When the cars' engines fell silent, the puppies rushed forward to greet the Dawsons and meet the visitors.

As Jeremy closed the door of the car, he felt Thunder's front paws on his legs. He pushed Thunder's paws to the ground and led him into the shade. "Come on, boy." When Jeremy sat down in the grass, Thunder climbed into his lap and began licking his face. All of a sudden, Thunder didn't care about meeting the visitors. Everything about Jeremy— his smell, his voice, and the way his hands and face felt—told Thunder that something was wrong. Jeremy was upset. He was sad, even a little afraid, and Thunder thought he knew why. These humans were here to pick out a dog, and that dog could be Thunder. He decided that, if he had to go home with the visitors, he would, but he would not volunteer. Let the other puppies go and meet the visitors. Thunder would stay with Jeremy for as long as he could. He sat down in Jeremy's lap and pressed his head against Jeremy's chest.

Sunny and Shadow, still eager to make friends with the visitors, could barely keep their front paws on the ground as they watched a man climb out of the car. As soon as they saw him, they knew that he was not like the other humans they had seen on the farm. His skin was wrinkled, not smooth like Jeremy's, and he moved a little more slowly than other humans they had seen. As they sniffed the air, they knew that he must be a good and kind man, for he smelled of peace and love. When he knelt down, they trotted toward him and sniffed and licked his outstretched hands. He scratched their ears and made soft and gentle sounds that the puppies knew must be human words. Although they could not understand the words, they could hear in them the same gentleness and friendliness that they had smelled in his scent.

The man used the car's bumper to steady himself as he stood up, and the puppies followed him to the other side of the car. He opened the door and held a woman's hand as she stepped out. The two puppies saw that she, too, moved a little slowly and had wrinkled skin, and they smelled in her the same peace and love that they had smelled in the man. They walked to her and sniffed her ankles. Evert brought a lawn chair, and the woman sat down. Sunny placed a forepaw on the edge of the chair, pulled herself up, and laid her head on the woman's knee. As the woman scratched Sunny's ears, she made sounds like the sounds her husband had made. Sunny didn't understand the sounds, but she thought they were the most wonderful sounds she'd ever heard.

The man looked at the two puppies and then at Evert. "These are mighty fine puppies, Evert, but didn't you say you had three?"

Evert looked around the yard. "Yes, I did say three. Oh, there's the third one, over there with Jeremy. Jeremy, let go of that puppy."

Jeremy took his hands off Thunder and held them in the air. "I'm not holding him, Daddy."

Evert knelt down. "Come on over here, pup, and say hello to Mrs. Haskin. Achilles, come on, boy."

Thunder understood the word *Achilles*, but not the rest of Evert's sounds. He thought Evert might be calling him to come meet the visitors. He thought that he ought to obey Evert, but his instinct told him that Jeremy needed him. He wasn't sure what he should do, so he pressed his head even harder against Jeremy's chest.

Audrey laughed. "Well, it looks like he's decided to be shy today. Isn't that cute?"

Evert walked to Jeremy and was about to take Thunder from his lap when Mrs. Haskin spoke up. "Well, that's okay. He's going to be a bigger dog than I want. Besides, I like this one. She has a happy face, and I like a dog with a happy face." She patted her knee, and Sunny hopped into her lap. "Yep," Mrs. Haskin laughed, "This is my dog, all right."

Right away, Thunder knew that Jeremy felt a little better. Mrs. Haskin gave Sunny a nudge, and Sunny jumped to the ground. As Mrs. Haskin stood up and climbed back into the car, Ginger trotted to Sunny and gave her a lick on the nose. "Well, Sunny, it looks like you have found your human. Take good care of her."

"I will, Mother," Sunny replied as Evert scooped her up and set her in Mrs. Haskin's lap. As the Haskins drove down the dirt driveway, Ginger and the puppies barked their goodbyes to Sunny.

16

As the sound of the Haskins' car faded into the distance, Jeremy lay on his back in the shade of the peach tree, smiling as he remembered the previous day's fishing trip. "Enjoy those you love while they're with you," his daddy had told him. Well, his best friend was still with him. Thunder might be gone in a little while, but Jeremy was tired of worrying and being sad. For now, he and his favorite puppy were together, and that was a reason to be happy and have fun.

Jeremy rolled onto his hands and knees, snorted like a bull, and charged toward Thunder, who was scratching his back on the grass a few feet away. Thunder rolled to his feet and met the charge by throwing his front paws onto Jeremy's shoulders and licking the back of Jeremy's neck. Jeremy fell flat and rolled over, and Thunder, no longer able to reach the back of Jeremy's neck, began licking Jeremy's face. Laughing so hard he nearly coughed, Jeremy pushed Thunder away as hard as he could. The puppy stumbled, and, before he could get up, Jeremy was standing. He picked up the old towel his mother had given to the puppies as a toy and dangled it in front of Thunder.

Thunder liked this game, and he was good at it. He lunged at the towel, caught it with his teeth, and began to tug as hard as he could. Jeremy, at the other end, tugged back but soon lost his grip and sat down in the grass with a thud while Thunder tumbled backward. Now that he had the towel all to himself, Thunder trotted toward Jeremy. When Jeremy reached for the towel, Thunder quickly ran away. When Jeremy tried to head him off, he darted in the other direction.

For several minutes, Thunder ran to and fro with Jeremy chasing him and trying to grab the towel. Thunder could easily have simply outrun Jeremy so that Jeremy never came close to him, but it was more fun to let Jeremy catch up and then change directions at the last second. Soon Thunder decided that even this was really no challenge. Tug-o-war was more fun. He turned to face Jeremy and let him grab the towel. To make sure that he would not lose his grip again, Jeremy rolled one corner of the towel into a narrow band and wrapped it around his right hand twice.

Jeremy soon started to think that losing his grip might not be so bad, for Thunder was now strong enough to yank Jeremy around the yard. Each time Thunder yanked on the towel, Jeremy pulled against him with all his might, and, each time, Jeremy found himself running in the direction of Thunder's tug. As Thunder yanked and Jeremy ran, suddenly, "Rrrrrriiiiiiiiip!" The towel ripped in two, leaving Jeremy lying on his back and Thunder holding a small corner of cloth.

Jeremy jumped to his feet. "Aha! Look what I've got, Achilles!" Still holding the towel in his right hand, he ran as fast he could around the house to the back yard. Thunder spat out the corner and gave chase. As Jeremy sped across the back yard toward the barn, he suddenly hit the ground, feeling as if his right arm had been nearly pulled from its socket. Lying on his side in the grass, he looked back to see Thunder sitting on his haunches, holding the other end of the towel in his teeth and wagging his tail. Jeremy grabbed his shoulder and let out a loud sound that was something between a laugh and a moan. When Thunder jumped onto his chest and began licking his face, the moaning gave way to loud, gleeful laughter.

Jeremy finally heard his mama's voice the third time she called his name. "Jeremy!"

"Ma'am?" Jeremy was still laughing so hard that he had a little trouble answering.

"Sweetie, you're going to have to bring the puppy around front now. There's a lady here looking for a dog."

"Well, the other puppy's around front. She can have him."

"Jeremy . . . she wants a big dog."

"Mama, the other puppy's going to be big. Not as big as Achilles, but still big."

"Jeremy. We've been through this. We're giving all the puppies away. If she wants this one, she can have him."

"But . . . . "

"Jeremy."

"Yes, Ma'am."

Jeremy sat up and pulled Thunder close to him. Thunder knew that Jeremy's mood had changed very quickly. His sadness and fear were back. The smell of a visitor drifting on the breeze from the front yard told Thunder why. Jeremy sighed deeply, stood up, and started toward the front yard. Thunder didn't want to follow, but he remembered what his mother had told him, and he knew it was the right thing to do. If it was the Father's plan for him to leave the farm, then he would leave. Besides, he wanted to stay close to Jeremy for as long as he could. If Jeremy was going to the front yard, Thunder was going with him.

When Jeremy and Thunder rounded the corner of the house and reached the front yard, they saw an old pick-up truck, much like J.L.'s, sitting at the end of the dirt driveway. Next to it, Shadow lay on his back in the grass, stretching and wagging his tail while the young woman kneeling beside him scratched his belly. She looked up at Evert and Audrey, smiling. "Friendly, gentle puppy you've got here. And he'll grow to be big and strong. Just what I'm looking for."

Evert nodded toward Jeremy and Thunder. "Well, there's the other one. You're welcome to take your pick."

When the woman saw Thunder, she chuckled warmly. "Oh, my goodness. I'm looking for a *big* dog, not a *giant* one. I think this one here is just about right. If it's all right with you, I'll take him and be on my way."

Audrey handed the woman Shadow's vet records. "He's all yours. I hope you enjoy him."

"I'm sure I will. Thank you very much." The woman picked Shadow up, set him in the passenger seat of her truck, and climbed into the driver's seat. Jeremy watched as the truck headed up the dirt driveway. "Who was that lady, Mama? I don't think I've ever seen her before."

"Her name's Penny Martin, Jeremy. I'd never met her before today. She lives just outside town, and she said she wanted a big, strong dog."

Jeremy scratched Thunder's ears. "Well, I'm glad she thought Achilles was too big. I guess I get to keep him a little longer, huh?"

"It looks that way Jeremy, but remember, we *will* find a home for him."

Jeremy looked up at his mama. "But if nobody wants him...."

"*Somebody* will, Jeremy. I'm sure there are still a lot of people out there who want puppies, and, the next time somebody comes here looking for one, Achilles will be the only one we have."

17

The next morning, after the Dawsons had finished breakfast, Jeremy went about his usual task of washing and drying the dishes. From the window above the sink, he could see Thunder running in tight circles, chasing his tail. A few times, he caught it in his teeth and then went staggering across the yard, as though pulling himself by his own tail. Jeremy laughed. "Well, I guess since he doesn't have any other puppies to chase now, he has to chase himself."

At that thought, Jeremy's face fell, and he sighed. "No other puppies." Thunder was the only puppy left, and, if things went according to Jeremy's parents' plan, soon he too would be gone. When he had finished the dishes, Jeremy hung up the towel and went out the back door. When Thunder heard the door shut, he forgot his game and rushed to greet Jeremy. Jeremy knelt in the grass, and Thunder threw his forepaws onto Jeremy's shoulders and began to lick his face. Suddenly, Jeremy pushed Thunder away, stood up, and ran toward the front yard. "Betcha can't catch me."

Both Thunder and Jeremy knew how this game would end, but that didn't take away any of the fun for either of them. Thunder eagerly gave chase. As they rounded the house into the front yard, he easily caught up with Jeremy and wrapped his front legs around Jeremy's ankles. Jeremy fell with a thud, and Thunder scampered onto his back and began licking his neck and ears. Jeremy laughed so hard that he didn't notice his mother's foot right next to his head. He had nearly landed on it when he fell. Then he heard her voice.

"Jeremy!"

"Ma'am?" Jeremy was still laughing so hard that it took him a couple of seconds to finish the word *Ma'am*.

"I'm glad the two of you are here." She nodded toward the dirt driveway.

When Jeremy stood up he saw a big, black car heading toward the yard. "Who's that, Mama?"

"I don't know, Jeremy, but there's a good chance it's somebody looking for a puppy. Achilles is the only one left, so unless they think he's too big . . . . Now, Sweetie, I know this is hard for you, but it's the way it has to be. I want you to try to be polite."

Jeremy felt his lower lip begin to quiver. Then, he had an idea. "Hmmm. Too big." This was no time to cry; Jeremy had work to do. He fell to the ground, rolled onto his back, and pulled Thunder onto his chest. When the car reached the edge of the yard, Thunder was standing on Jeremy, licking his face. Jeremy laughed so hard that he screamed; in fact, a stranger would have thought that Jeremy was in pain.

The door of the big, black car opened, and out stepped a tall, well-dressed woman with gray hair. She looked at Jeremy and Thunder for a moment, and then she looked at Audrey. "Hello. You must be Mrs. Dawson."

"Yes, I'm Audrey Dawson, and this is my son Jeremy. Jeremy! Stop screaming and get up!"

"Yes, Ma'am." Jeremy stood up and greeted the woman.

The woman eyed Thunder. "I'm Kathryn Waldren. I understand you have some puppies to give away. My grandson comes to visit for a few weeks every summer, and it occurred to me yesterday that it might be nice if I had a dog for him to play with."

Audrey smiled. "Well, you got here just in time. We only have one left. If you like him, you're welcome to take him home with you."

Mrs. Waldren eyed Thunder and raised an eyebrow. "I must have misread your sign. I thought the puppies were only eight weeks old."

Audrey smiled. "You read it right, Mrs. Waldren. He's eight weeks and a few days."

Mrs. Waldren gasped. "Only eight weeks? My word! He must weight 30 or 35 pounds! He'll be huge."

Jeremy laughed. "Yes, Ma'am! He sure will be! Just look at these paws; they're bigger than my hands!"

Mrs. Waldren's eyes widened. "So I see."

"He's strong, too. He can knock me down with no trouble at all."

Audrey stammered a bit, trying to find the right words. "He's . . . he's really a sweet puppy, Mrs. Waldren."

Jeremy knelt beside Thunder and squeezed him tightly so that the puppy wriggled powerfully, pulling Jeremy down as he broke free. "He sure is! He's very sweet, and he loves to play. Your grandson will love him. One of his favorite things to do is to jump on my chest and lick my face, but he always lets me up when I start to choke."

Mrs. Waldren took a step toward the big, black car. Jeremy stood up and brushed his shirt. "And you don't have to worry too much about the mess. Mama says it's usually pretty easy to get the mud and the puppy spit out of my clothes."

Mrs. Waldren laughed. "Well, I have a little practice in that area myself. If my grandson were as big as you, this puppy might be perfect for him, but he's only four. He needs a smaller dog . . . and so do I. Thank you, Mrs. Dawson. Ya'll have a nice day."

As the big, black car headed up the dirt driveway, Jeremy sighed. "Well, I guess he'll just have to wait a little longer to get a home, the poor little thing."

Audrey felt the corners of her mouth begin to move upward. She bit her lips, covered her mouth, and began to shake. She took a deep breath and let it out slowly. When she had stopped shaking, she spoke. "Jeremy Dawson!"

"Ma'am?"

Audrey closed her eyes and took another deep breath. She felt herself begin to shake again. "Go play!"

"Yes, Ma'am."

When Jeremy and Thunder had disappeared into the back yard, Audrey went into the house, buried her face in a sofa pillow, and laughed.

18

The next day was library day. Every Tuesday morning during the summer, Jeremy's mama took him to the library to return the book he had just read and get a new one. Usually, Jeremy checked out an adventure story, like *Pecos Bill*, or a book about a real-life hero. He had just finished reading about Daniel Boone. Jeremy liked reading about adventure. He liked to imagine what it would be like to live in another place and another time, to drive cattle across the plains or lead settlers on the frontier. But today, Jeremy was after something different.

As he and his mother approached the library door, Jeremy felt a strong hand grab his arm and squeeze. "Where you goin', boy?" asked a gruff voice behind him. Jeremy was about to cry out for help, but the laughter he saw in his mother's eyes took away his fear. When he turned to look at the man behind him, he let out some loud laughter of his own.

"Hey, Mr. McClaren!" Jeremy shouted.

"Hey there, Partner," said the tall, gray-haired man. "I saw you eatin' those ribs at church on Sunday. Did you get enough?"

"I could never get enough of those ribs," Jeremy answered. "But I ate a lot of them, and they were good!"

"Well, I'll tell you what," Mr. McClaren said, kneeling in front of Jeremy with a big grin on his face. "You and your mama and daddy will just have to come to my house one evening, and we'll see if we can't fill you up with ribs." He winked his eye and gave Jeremy a gentle poke on the shoulder.

Jeremy looked up at his mother with wide eyes. "Can we, Mama?"

"Sure we can, Honey," Audrey said, "but right now we'd better go ahead and get you a book."

"Oh yeah," Jeremy said, suddenly remembering the reason he had come to the library. "See you later, Mr. McClaren," he shouted over his shoulder as he headed into the library. "I gotta get a dog training book."

"That boy sure is growing up fast," Mr. McClaren chuckled. "You ought to be proud of him."

"He's a good boy," Audrey said, "and smart, too. Looks like he's decided he wants to train the last of Ginger's puppies."

"I hear ol' Ginger had a fine litter."

"That she did," said Audrey. "And I think the last one may be the finest of them all. No one's taken him yet, because he's going to be huge, but we can't keep him. Say, you like big dogs, Lloyd. Couldn't you use one now to keep an eye on your place?"

Mr. McClaren sighed a long, deep sigh. "Well, when ol' Major died, I said I wasn't going to have any more dogs."

Audrey nodded. "Yes, Major was a great dog, and you had him for a long time. I know it broke your heart when he died."

"I'll tell you what," Mr. McClaren answered. "It was about as bad as losing a young'n. I said I wouldn't have another dog, but, you know, sometimes that yard seems awful empty."

"Well," Audrey smiled, "if you decide you want another dog, we have just the one, and you're welcome to him."

Mr. McClaren squinted one eye and nodded. "I'll keep that in mind, Audrey. I sure will."

"Well, it's always nice to see you, Lloyd," Audrey said as she opened the library door. "Give Joyce a hug for me."

When Jeremy heard his mother come into the library, he was already busy scanning the shelves of "how-to" books. After a few seconds, he saw *The Big Book of Dog Training*. "Ah!" Jeremy thought. "Just what I need." Then, when he pulled it off the shelf and began to thumb through it, he realized that *The Big Book of Dog Training* really was a *big* book. It was almost three hundred pages long, and, when Jeremy tried to read a little, he saw some words he had never seen before. "It would take me forever to read all this," he thought.

He started to put the book back onto the shelf, and then he remembered that only Miss Terri, the librarian, was allowed to reshelve books. That was Miss Terri's way of making sure all the books were in the right places so people could find them. Jeremy carried *The Big Book of Dog Training* to a nearby reading table, set it down, and then went back to the area where the "how-to" books were shelved. As he searched the shelves and thumbed through books, Jeremy saw that the library had more than two dozen books about dog training. Some were very thick, and some were thin. Some had lots of big words; some had mostly small words. Some had lots of pictures; some had only a few. Some were about training *and caring for* dogs; some were only about *training* dogs. Some were about training dogs *and other pets*; some were only about training *dogs*. Jeremy heaved a big sigh, sat down on the floor, and rested his chin in his hands.

"You look like you could use a hand, Jeremy," came a soft whisper from behind him. "Can I help?" It was Miss Terri.

Jeremy looked over his shoulder. "I sure hope so, Miss Terri. I'm looking for a book about training dogs, and I don't know which one I should get."

"Well, maybe I can help. Hmmmmm. Training dogs. Let's see." Miss Terri's lips tightened and twisted a little as her eyes moved from book to book. Finally, she spoke. "Ah! How 'bout this one, Jeremy?" She took a book from the shelf and held it out to Jeremy. "It's really meant for someone a little older than you, but you do a lot of reading, and you're good at it. I think you can handle it."

Jeremy took the book from Miss Terri's hand and looked at the cover. "*The Boy's Guide to Training His Dog*," he read. Jeremy thumbed through the book. It was only about 100 pages long, and it had plenty of pictures to show him how to do the things the words described. He knew almost all the words he saw, and he knew that he could look up the others in his dictionary.

"This looks like a good one, Miss Terri. I'll take it."

19

That afternoon, Jeremy fed the chickens and weeded the flower beds faster than he ever had. After he had dumped the weeds onto the brush pile, he rushed into the barn, rummaged through an old cardboard box, and found an old leash and training collar. He took the collar and leash to the back porch and hung them on a nail beside the back door. Now, he had only one thing left to do. He ran to his room, grabbed *The Boy's Guide to Training His Dog*, and sat down on his bed. By the time his daddy came home for supper, Jeremy had finished two of the book's ten chapters. He wanted to keep reading, but he knew his mama wouldn't let him skip supper. Besides, he could smell fresh cornbread, and he loved cornbread almost as much as he loved chicken and yellow rice. So he marked his place, closed the book, and went into the bathroom to wash up.

From the bathroom, he could hear his parents talking. He couldn't understand everything they said, but he caught something about the library and training dogs. His mama sounded a little worried, so Jeremy was a little nervous as he took his seat at the table. After his daddy had given thanks, Jeremy helped himself to some ham, green beans, and cornbread and then set out to eat his supper almost as fast as he had fed the chickens.

"Jeremy!" his mama said. "Don't eat so fast. You'll choke."

"What's your hurry, son?" asked his daddy.

"I cab a noo boo," Jeremy answered through a mouthful of ham, cornbread, and maybe a few beans.

"Try that again when your mouth's empty, young'n," his daddy said.

Jeremy chewed some more, swallowed, and took a sip of iced tea. "Sorry, Daddy. I have a new book, and I want to get back to reading it."

"That book's not going anywhere, son. You have plenty of time to read it. I'm glad you like to read, but reading doesn't excuse bad table manners."

"Yessir. It's just that I'm reading a book about training dogs, and I want to read as much as I can tonight, so I can start training Achilles tomorrow."

Evert looked at Audrey, and she looked back the way she always did when she was worried.

Evert smiled at Jeremy. "So, you want to make sure whoever takes Achilles gets a well-trained dog, huh?"

Jeremy looked down for a second and then raised his head. "Well, Daddy, you told me that I should enjoy my friends while they were with me. Achilles is with me now, and I don't know how much longer he'll be here. I'm just trying to have as much fun with him as I can before he leaves."

Evert was silent for a moment. Then he spoke. "Jeremy, you know that we're going to give that puppy away, right?

You're not thinking that, if you train him, we'll let you keep him, are you?"

Jeremy took a sip of tea to give himself time to think. The truth was that he really didn't know the answer to his daddy's question. For a boy like Jeremy, hope doesn't go away easily. It's no easier to get rid of than a pesky fly. No matter how many times he swats it away, it just comes back. Jeremy was trying, really trying, to know for sure that his favorite puppy was going to leave, but he just couldn't help hoping that his parents would change their minds. And if the training changed their minds, that would be all right with Jeremy. But even if he'd had no hope at all, Jeremy still would have wanted to train the puppy and have fun with him. So he was being as truthful as he could when he said, "I know we have to give Achilles away, Daddy. I just want to have some fun with him while I can."

Evert smiled a half-smile. "Well, I guess that's a good idea. Finish eating your supper—like a person with manners, not like a pig—and then you can go back to your room and read some more."

"Yessir. Thanks, Daddy."

Jeremy finished eating as fast as he could without being rude, and then he excused himself.

After Jeremy had gone to his room, Audrey spoke. "Evert, do you think it's a good idea for him to be training that puppy? You know how attached to him he already is."

Evert washed down a bite of cornbread with a sip of tea. "Well, I did tell him he ought to enjoy his friends while he could. If I really believe what I said, I have to say he ought to have as much fun with the dog as he can before we find a home for the dog. That's just what he's doing."

Audrey sighed. "I just don't want Jeremy to be heart-broken."

"No way to stop that now. When that dog goes, Jeremy's going to be heart-broken—no way around it. We may as well let him have his fun while he can. It'll give him something good to remember later on."

"Do you think he's telling the truth, or is he really hoping to change our minds?"

"Who knows? Even he may not know for sure. But, either way, I think we should let him have his fun while he can."

"I hope you're right."

Evert swallowed his last sip of tea. "So do I."

20

The next morning, as soon as Jeremy had finished putting away the breakfast dishes, he quickly fed the chickens and then got the collar and leash from the back porch. He had read a little less than half of *The Boy's Guide to Training His Dog*, but he had already learned enough from it to make a good start. When Jeremy came around the corner of the house, Thunder was lying in the grass enjoying the morning sun. When he saw Jeremy coming, he stood up, stretched, yawned, and trotted to Jeremy's side. He quickly noticed that Jeremy was carrying some things Thunder hadn't seen before, and that made Thunder curious.

As Thunder sniffed at the strange objects, Jeremy formed the shorter one into a loop and slipped it over Thunder's ears and down to his neck. Thunder had never worn anything around his neck before, and he wasn't sure whether or not he liked it. Before Thunder could make up his mind, Jeremy attached the longer object to the shorter one and gave it a gentle tug.

At that point, Thunder made up his mind: he did not like this one bit. He was confused. Had he somehow angered Jeremy again? Jeremy didn't smell angry, but Thunder couldn't understand why he was doing this. Thunder loved Jeremy and trusted him, but, like all living creatures, he liked being free, and this thing Jeremy had attached to him made him feel like a prisoner. Thunder tugged and jerked, first in one direction and then in another, pulling Jeremy to the ground. Then he rose onto his hind legs and pawed at the long thing. Afraid that the puppy would hurt himself, Jeremy let go of the long thing.

Thunder wasn't sure what to do now. He wanted to run away as fast as he could, but he also wanted always to stay with Jeremy. Wagging his tail, Thunder walked to Jeremy, who was lying on his back in the grass, and licked his face. Jeremy sat up and rolled onto his knees. He wrapped his arms around Thunder's neck and made gentle sounds. Thunder, of course, couldn't understand the sounds, except for the one sound that he had learned, the name *Achilles*. But the tone of Jeremy's voice, Jeremy's smell, and the feel of Jeremy's skin told him that Jeremy was happy and meant no harm. Thunder decided to go along with whatever Jeremy was doing.

Jeremy stood up, held the long thing, and walked back and forth across the yard. Thunder walked next to Jeremy, and Jeremy's sounds and smells let Thunder know that Jeremy was pleased. Thunder still didn't understand. He was happy to walk next to Jeremy. Jeremy didn't have to make him do it by wrapping something around his neck. Then, Jeremy stopped walking. When Thunder felt himself reach the end of the long thing, he stopped too. Jeremy made a sound and then pushed downward on Thunder's hind end as he pulled upward with the long thing. Thunder sat down. Jeremy made many happy sounds as he stroked Thunder's back and chest. Thunder knew that he had pleased Jeremy; that made Thunder happy.

Then Jeremy tugged a little and started walking again. When Thunder felt Jeremy's tug, he started walking too. Once again, when Jeremy stopped, Thunder stopped. Again, Jeremy made the sound, pushed downward, and pulled upward. Again, Thunder sat. As before, Jeremy made happy sounds and stroked Thunder. Once more, Jeremy began to walk, and Thunder walked with him. Jeremy stopped, and Thunder stopped. By now, Thunder knew the sound—*Sit!*—and he thought it must be a word. This time, when Jeremy said the word, Thunder sat, without waiting for the upward pull or the downward push. Jeremy sounded even happier than before as he stroked Thunder and scratched his ears.

Now, Thunder was starting to understand what Jeremy was doing. Jeremy was teaching Thunder to understand some human words and to know what Jeremy wanted him to do. This could make Jeremy and Thunder even better friends than they already were, and Thunder liked that idea. He listened closely to Jeremy and tried hard to understand Jeremy's words and obey them. Over the next few weeks, Thunder learned several new words and even phrases: *heel, stay, down, come on, roll over.* Thunder's favorite phrase, the phrase he really loved to hear, was the phrase that told him that he had made Jeremy happy: *Good boy, Achilles! Good boy!*

21

Good Boy, Achilles! Good Boy! Thunder heard that phrase many times over the next several months. And he heard it from Jeremy, because he stayed on the Dawsons' farm much longer than anyone had expected. For a couple of weeks, it seemed like almost every day someone stopped by the farm looking for a puppy. But they all said things like, "He's just a little too big," or, "My yard's just a little too small." Then people stopped by less and less often. After a while, they stopped coming.

So Thunder stayed on the farm. He was there in August, when Jeremy started school again, and he learned to walk Jeremy to the bus stop in the morning and meet him there in the afternoon. He was there in October, when the leaves fell, and he and Jeremy rolled and wrestled in the crunchy piles. He was there in December, when the Dawsons celebrated Christmas, and Jeremy gave him a piece of rawhide for chewing and a brand new rope for playing tug-o-war.

And he was there on a cold, clear day in January. It was Jeremy's first day back in school after Christmas break, and Thunder was lying at the edge of the yard, enjoying the sunshine. As the days had grown colder, his coat had grown thicker, so, even though the air was cold, Thunder felt fine. Around mid-afternoon, when he heard the distant rumble of the school bus, Thunder stood, stretched, and took off at a trot toward the hard road. When the bus hissed to a stop at the end of the old, dirt driveway, Thunder was there, waiting for Jeremy.

"Good boy, Achilles!" Jeremy laughed as he scampered down the steps and hopped onto the dirt driveway. After stopping to scratch Thunder's ears, he started toward the house. "Hey, have you heard the news?" Jeremy asked as the two strode down the driveway. "They say it's going to snow tonight! A lot! You've never seen snow before, and I've only seen a little, but they say we're going to get a lot of it tonight! We're going to have us some fun! Man! I wish I had a sled; you could pull me on it. Oh well. Ooh! Maybe we can build a snowman . . . or a fort!"

Thunder didn't understand anything Jeremy was saying, but he knew Jeremy was very happy, and that made Thunder happy. Jeremy was so busy making plans for the snow that he didn't notice the sound of the engine behind them, but Thunder did. He pressed his shoulder against Jeremy's thigh and pushed. He weighed nearly seventy pounds now and could easily knock Jeremy down, so he was careful not to push too hard. Jeremy laughed as he staggered sideways. He thought Thunder was just playing, but then he saw the big, red pick-up truck roll past them and continue down the driveway.

As the truck passed, the driver chuckled and waved at Jeremy. He was very careful and would never have hit Jeremy or Thunder with his truck, but moving out of the way was a good idea all the same. Jeremy watched the truck for a moment; then his eyes grew wide. "Mr. McClaren!" Jeremy shot down the driveway, running as fast as his heavy coat would allow, with Thunder loping along beside him. By the time they reached the yard, Mr. McClaren was already out of the truck and talking with Evert and Audrey. "Mr. McClaren!" Jeremy shouted again as he came to a stop in front of his friend.

"Hello there, Partner!" Mr. McClaren said. "Long time no see. Put'er there!"

Jeremy grasped Mr. McClaren's hand and squeezed as hard as he could.

"Owww! Let go! Man, you're getting strong, Feller," Mr. McClaren moaned. Jeremy laughed.

"Hey, look here what I've got for you," Mr. McClaren said as he opened the door of his pick-up truck and took a big plastic bag off of the seat.

Right away, Jeremy knew what was in the bag. "Boiled peanuts! Thanks, Mr. McClaren!" Jeremy loved boiled peanuts, and Mr. McClaren grew and boiled the best peanuts around. Jeremy took the bag and ran to his mama. "Look, Mama! Boiled peanuts! Mama, have you heard the big news. It's going to snow tonight!"

Audrey smiled. "Yes, Jeremy, I've heard," she said softly. "But there's something we need to talk about." Jeremy noticed that his mama was looking over his shoulder, and he turned around to see Mr. McClaren kneeling in front of Thunder, looking carefully at his ears and teeth. Jeremy started toward the man and the dog. "How do you like my dog, Mr. McClaren? He's a beauty, isn't he?"

"He sure is, Jeremy," Mr. McClaren replied.

"His name's Achilles," Jeremy smiled.

"Achilles?" Mr. McClaren chuckled. "Well, that's too much for an old feller like me to remember. I think I'll name him Sam."

Jeremy stopped. "You'll name him? Daddy, is Mr. McClaren . . . ?"

Jeremy couldn't finish his sentence, so Evert interrupted. "Mr. McClaren's looking for a big dog to keep an eye on his house and barn, Jeremy."

"And I think this one will do just fine," said Mr. McClaren. "I'll take him."

Jeremy forgot about the snow and dropped the boiled peanuts. He jumped to Thunder's side, fell to his knees, and wrapped his arms around the dog's neck. Thunder knew that Jeremy was very unhappy, and he thought he knew why. Jeremy looked up at Mr. McClaren with a wrinkled brow and clenched teeth. "You can't have him," he cried. "He's mine, and his name's Achilles."

"Jeremy!" Evert shouted his son's name and then spoke more quietly. "We've talked about this already. You knew this was going to happen, and now it's time. Mr. McClaren's taking this puppy."

"Oh, now look here, little buddy," said Mr. McClaren, placing his hand on Jeremy's shoulder. "I didn't mean to . . . ."

"Lloyd," Evert interrupted. "We really do have to give this dog away. Don't let Jeremy talk you out of it."

Jeremy looked up at his daddy with tears running down both cheeks. "Please, Daddy . . . ."

"Jeremy," Evert said softly. "It's time to say goodbye."

Jeremy squeezed Thunder tightly and rubbed his face against the puppy's ear. "Goodbye, Achilles," he sobbed. "I love you. I'll never forget you. You be a good dog for Mr. McClaren. Okay?"

Thunder didn't understand what Jeremy was saying, but he knew what was happening. He turned to Jeremy and licked him from his Adam's apple to the top of his forehead, and then he pressed his head against Jeremy's chest. As Jeremy squeezed Thunder, he felt his daddy's hands on his shoulders.

"Come on, Jeremy," Evert said. "Let go of Achilles." Jeremy let go of Thunder and rose to his feet, wiping his eyes and sniffling.

"Take good care of him, Mr. McClaren," he said, nearly whispering. "He's a good dog."

"You better believe I will, Jeremy," said Mr. McClaren, wiping his eye. "Thank you for the puppy. You come visit him any time you want."

While Evert, Mr. McClaren, and Jeremy waited for Audrey to bring Thunder's vet records, Ginger stepped quietly to Thunder's side. Thunder hung his head and then, breathing deeply, held it high. "Well, Mother," he said with a shaky voice. "It looks like I have found my human."

"It does look that way," Ginger replied.

"I'll take good care of him, Mother."

"I know you will."

"If this is the Father's plan," Thunder said, "I know it's good. But it surely hurts."

When Audrey returned with Thunder's records, Mr. McClaren lowered his tailgate and gave it a tap, and Thunder jumped into the bed of the truck. "Come on, Sam," Mr. McClaren said. "Let's go home."

Ginger watched as the truck rattled back up the driveway. "The Father's plan," she whispered. "I wonder."

22

As Mr. McClaren's truck rumbled down the hard road, Thunder lay on a blanket in the truck bed to escape the cold wind. After only a few minutes, he felt the truck slow down, veer to the right, and come to a stop. When he stood up, he saw a friendly-looking little house with a hedge very much like the one at the Dawsons' house. On one side of the house stood a big oak tree that was sure to provide plenty of shade during the hot summer. On the other side stood a tea olive bush with new flowers on it. Behind the house and a little to the right stood a small barn. Through the open door, Thunder could see a lawn mower and a tractor. A six-foot fence surrounded both the house and the barn. When Mr. McClaren blew the horn, Mrs. McClaren hurried from the house and opened the big gate so that Mr. McClaren could drive into the yard.

Once the truck was stopped and the gate was closed, Mr. McClaren climbed out of the cab, and he and Mrs. McClaren began stroking Thunder's back, scratching his ears, and speaking softly to him. Thunder, of course, couldn't understand what they were saying, but from their smells and sounds and the way their skin felt when they touched him, he could tell that they were friendly and meant to treat him kindly. He liked them. Then Mr. McClaren lowered the tailgate. "Come on, Sam," he said. Thunder understood *come on*, although he didn't understand the rest of what Mr. McClaren had said. He hopped out of the truck bed and followed Mr. and Mrs. McClaren toward the house. "Come on, Sam," Mr. McClaren repeated. "Good boy, Sam." Now, Thunder understood. *Sam* was Mr. McClaren's name for him.

"It doesn't sound as good as *Achilles*," Thunder thought, "But I guess it's my true name. I'd better learn to answer to it."

Thunder followed the McClarens around the house, through the back yard, and into the barn. In one corner of the barn, Mr. McClaren piled up some straw to make a soft, warm bed for him. Mrs. McClaren brought him two big dishes, one filled with water and the other with food. Thunder tasted a little of the food. It was different from the food the Dawsons had fed him, but it tasted good all the same. Then Mr. McClaren took a collar off a shelf and fastened it around Thunder's neck. When the McClarens headed toward the house, Thunder ran after them. He nudged the back of Mr. McClaren's leg with his nose, and when Mr. McClaren turned around, Thunder dropped his chest to the ground, wagged his tail high in the air, and barked a friendly, playful bark. Mr. McClaren chuckled, bent over to scratch Thunder's ears, and then turned and walked toward the house. Thunder ran around him and sat down in front of him, ears pricked and tail wagging.

"Well, Lloyd," laughed Mrs. McClaren, "I'm going inside, but I think you have to stay out here a little while."

"I think you're right, Joyce," Mr. McClaren answered. "Okay, Sam, let's play!"

Mr. McClaren looked around the yard and found a nice, strong stick. He showed it to Thunder and threw it as far as he could. Almost as soon as the stick hit the ground, Thunder picked it up and raced back to Mr. McClaren. When Mr. McClaren reached for the stick, Thunder yanked it away and ran a few steps.

"Oh, you want to play chase, do you?" asked Mr. McClaren. "Well, sorry, boy, I'm a little old for that."

Thunder didn't understand what Mr. McClaren was saying, but he could see that his new human wasn't going to chase him, so he ran back to Mr. McClaren and let him grab the stick. Then he began to pull, and Mr. McClaren let go. That was no fun for Thunder, so he let Mr. McClaren grab the stick again, and this time Thunder let go.

"Good boy, Sam!" Mr. McClaren said. "Good boy!"

Now, Thunder understood what Mr. McClaren wanted him to do. Again, Mr. McClaren threw the stick as far as he could, and again Thunder grabbed it and brought it back. Thunder had never played this game with Jeremy, but he liked it, so every time Mr. McClaren threw the stick, Thunder fetched it. After several throws, a strong wind that felt like ice-cold water began to whistle through the trees and the fence, and Mr. McClaren gave Thunder a rub on the neck and went into the house. In spite of his thick coat, the icy wind made Thunder cold, so he trotted to the barn and nestled down in the warm bed of straw. Outside, the sun was low in the sky, and thick clouds were rolling in from the north like an invading army of cotton balls. In the east, the sky was already dark. In the west, the sun seemed to be setting the clouds ablaze, but the flames were slowly dying as the sun sank into the horizon.

Curled up in the straw, Thunder lay deep in thought for a long time. He thought about his new collar. On the Dawsons' farm, Thunder had worn a collar only when Jeremy was training him, and this one made him itch a little. But he thought he could get used to it.

He thought about his bed of straw. It was soft and warm, and inside the barn he was protected from the wind. It reminded him of the pile of straw in the Dawsons' barn. He knew he would sleep well and feel fine in his new bed, even in very harsh weather.

He thought about the McClarens' yard. It was shady, much like the Dawsons' yard, and even though it was surrounded by a fence, which seemed new and strange to Thunder, he had plenty of room to run and play.

He thought about Mr. and Mrs. McClaren. They both seemed to be kind and gentle humans, much like Evert and Audrey Dawson. They had given him food and water, and they had scratched his ears. Mr. McClaren had even taught him a new game. The Father had given him good humans and a good home.

In fact, his new home was very much like his old home, but it was also very different. Thunder missed Ginger, of course, but he had known all his life that puppies must grow up and leave their mothers. So, even though it made him sad, being away from her somehow seemed right.

What seemed wrong, so wrong that he thought it could never seem right, was being away from Jeremy. Thunder knew that the Father's plan was good and that it was his duty to take care of the humans the Father had given him. He planned to do his duty, even if it meant giving up his life. Still, he couldn't stop thinking about Jeremy; he couldn't stop wanting to be with Jeremy. Lying in that pile of straw in the McClarens' barn, Thunder felt very, very alone. He began to whimper. He tried to be quiet, but he couldn't stop himself. Soon he was yelping so loudly that he thought everyone in the county must hear him.

Suddenly, through the doorway of the barn he saw a light on the McClarens' back porch. He heard the screen door creek, and then he saw a figure coming toward the barn. When the figure reached the barn, he saw that it was Mrs. McClaren, dressed in a heavy coat and thick, fuzzy slippers. She sat down on an upside down wash tub next to the pile of straw and began to stroke Thunder's back.

"Don't cry, Sam," she said, almost singing the words like a lullaby. "It's okay. I know you miss your mama and your friends, but Lloyd and I love you very much, and we're going to take very good care of you. Everything will be all right, sweetie." Thunder didn't understand what she was saying, but the love in her voice and in her touch made him feel better. He rolled onto his back, and Mrs. McClaren began to rub his belly, just like Jeremy used to. He let out a long, deep sigh, rolled onto his shoulder, and laid his head on Mrs. McClaren's fuzzy slipper. As Mrs. McClaren stroked his ears and spoke in her soft voice, Thunder felt the Father's love surround him. He began to think that, although he would always love Jeremy, he might grow to love the McClarens just as much. He might be very happy living at their house and taking care of them.

Mrs. McClaren stroked Thunder's ears until she began to tremble from the cold. When she slid her slipper out from under his head, Thunder stretched and yawned but did not open his eyes. As she walked back to the house, the first flakes of snow began to drift like feathers to the ground.

23

"We've got a lot of snow on the ground, this morning, folks," the voice on the radio said. "As much as six inches in a few places. It wouldn't seem like much to my cousins up north, but for this area, that is a whole *heap* of snow."

Jeremy squinted and rubbed his eyes with both fists. Then, he opened them wide. "Snow!" he whispered. He kicked off the covers, jumped out of bed, and leapt to the window. This time he shouted. "Snow!" He threw on his heavy coat, pulled on his boots, and ran into the hall. "Mama! Daddy! Have you seen the snow?" Without waiting for an answer, he ran out the back door; half jumped, half slid down the steps; and set to work making a snowball. Laughing, he looked around the yard. "Hey, Achill...."

Jeremy let the snow fall from his hands and sat down on the bottom step. The cold slush soaked into his pajama pants, but he didn't care. He didn't care about snowballs; he didn't care about snowmen; he didn't care about snow forts. Achilles was gone; nothing else mattered. Ginger trotted to the bottom of the steps, sat down in front of Jeremy, and laid her paw on his knee. He reached out and scratched her ear, and she licked his nose. "You're a good doggie, Ginger," Jeremy said in a shaky whisper. Then he sat with his face in his hands until his mama opened the door behind him.

"Jeremy! What are you doing sitting there in the snow like that? You'll catch pneumonia, honey. Jeremy?"

Jeremy didn't move. "Achilles is gone, Mama."

Audrey wiped her eye, stepped down, and stood beside him. "I know, sweetie, and I know it hurts. I miss him too. But right now you have to get ready for school. Come on."

Audrey took his hand and pulled gently, but hard enough to let him know she meant it. Jeremy stood up, his pajama pants crackling a little as they pulled free from the slush that had stuck to them. Audrey wrapped her arms around him and kissed him on top of the head, and the two went inside.

When Jeremy had finished dressing, he went to the kitchen and sat down with Evert to eat breakfast. Soon Audrey came to the table with a platter of pancakes and sausage. "Guess what, Jeremy," she said as she sat down. "The man on the radio says your school's closed today because of the snow. How 'bout that? You can stay home and play in the snow today. Maybe you and I can have a snowball fight."

"Okay, maybe," Jeremy mumbled.

After Evert had given thanks, the family ate breakfast. Evert talked about the cold weather and the tractor he planned to repair that day. "I don't like working with gloves on," he said, "but I think I'll have to wear them today."

Audrey talked about the quilt she was making for the county quilt show. "I found some really nice fabric," she said. "I think I have a good chance at the blue ribbon this year."

Jeremy didn't talk about anything at all, and he ate only one sausage patty and a few bites of a pancake. After breakfast, he went to his room and fell onto his bed. Through the window, he could see the snow stretching into the distance like a soft, glittery blanket. "Who cares about the snow?" he sighed. "Achilles is gone." He tried to ignore the knock on the door, but then he heard his mother's voice.

"Jeremy, it's Mama. I'm coming in."

The door opened and Audrey stepped into the room.

"You're not going stay in your room and mope all day, son. Just lying there thinking about Achilles will only make it worse. You need to get your mind on something else. Besides, we hardly ever get snow like this around here. Why, it may be 20 years before it happens again. If you don't get out there and enjoy it, you may regret it for the rest of your life."

The tone of Audrey's voice told Jeremy that arguing with his mama wouldn't do any good. He slid from his bed onto the floor; pulled on his heavy coat, his boots, his gloves, and his warm cap; and dragged himself into the hallway.

"Go on," Audrey insisted. "Get on out there."

Jeremy trudged out the back door and down the steps. After he had taken about ten steps into the yard, he felt something cold and slushy hit him in the back of the head. He turned around to see his mama laughing and pointing at him.

"Awww, Mama!" he whined. Before he finished his words, his mouth filled with snow as another snowball hit him in the face. Still laughing, Audrey ran and hid behind the oak tree. She peeked around the trunk and stuck out her tongue.

"All right," Jeremy laughed. "If you want a war, I'll give you one!"

He scooped up some snow, formed a ball, and charged toward the tree and his mama. Just as he tossed his frozen cannon ball, Audrey ducked behind the tree, and the snowball sailed past her. When Jeremy stooped to pick up more snow, he felt a cold, heavy clump hit him in the back. When he turned, he saw his mama skipping around the corner of the house, teasing him, "Nya-nya-nya-nya-nya."

This called for a sneaky plan. Jeremy ran a few steps after his mother to make her think he was chasing her. Then he doubled back. As fast as he could, he made two snowballs and knelt behind the oak tree, waiting for his mama to finish her trip around the house. After a second or two, he saw her skip around the corner, looking behind her. When she was close enough, he popped out from his hiding place, still kneeling, and fired his frosty rockets, one right after the other. The first missed, but the second found its mark.

"Ha!" Jeremy shouted. "Caught in an ambush."

"Aaaaargh!" With snow clinging to her coat and dripping from her hair, Audrey let out a shout and rushed at Jeremy. Just as he turned to run, she caught him, laid him gently on his back in the snow, and began to tickle him. Jeremy bounced with laughter as he tossed fistfuls of snow at his mama's head. Finally, Audrey stopped tickling, and she and Jeremy sat together in the snow, catching their breath.

"Look at us," Audrey said. "We're both soaking wet. We'd better go change clothes."

"Aw, Mama," Jeremy protested. "I want to play some more."

"You're welcome to come back out and play, Jeremy. But first you have to get out of those wet things."

Jeremy changed clothes and then spent the rest of the day playing in the snow. He made a small snowman in the front yard, and then he knocked its head off with snowballs. He thought it was probably bad manners to have a headless snowman in the front yard, so he gave it a new head. After a quick lunch, he found out that an old garbage can lid made a pretty good downhill sled. That evening, the Dawsons had chili for supper, and Jeremy ate two bowlfuls and three pieces of cornbread. He was so hungry he didn't even mind the beans much.

When his bedtime came, Jeremy went to his room and sank into his bed, exhausted. "Mama was right," he thought. "It was good to go out and play instead of just sitting around thinking about Achilles."

Out in the yard, a prowling raccoon prowled too close to the chicken pen, and Ginger chased him away. In his room, Jeremy heard her bark, and he almost expected to hear Thunder join her. The strange sound of one dog barking rather than two reminded Jeremy how lonely he was. "I wish I could go back out and play some more," he thought. "Because now I can't stop thinking about him."

As Jeremy's tears rolled down his cheek and onto his pillow, he began to sniffle and then to shake. All of a sudden, he rolled off his bed and walked on tiptoe to his closet. Careful not to let his parents know he was out of bed, he opened the closet door, moved his baseball bat to one side, and took out his backpack. He packed up some warm clothing, his flashlight, his pocket knife, some matches for starting fires, a magnifying glass in case he ran out of matches, and his sleeping bag—everything he thought he would need for getting along in the woods. His tent would make the pack too heavy, so he would have to sleep under the stars. He pushed the pack under his bed, changed into a pair of blue jeans and a flannel shirt, climbed back into bed, and waited with the covers pulled up around his neck. When his mama opened his door to check on him just before she and his daddy went to bed, she saw her son lying under the covers with his eyes closed.

Jeremy waited until he was sure his parents were asleep. Then, he climbed out of his bed; pulled on his boots, his heavy coat, his gloves, and his warm cap; and opened his window. He didn't want his backpack to hit the ground with a thud. That would be sure to wake Ginger, who was sleeping in the barn to stay out of the cold wind. If she knew he was leaving, she would try to stop him, and her barking would wake his parents. So he used a short piece of rope to lower the pack to the ground. Then he grabbed his fishing pole and leaned it against the wall just outside the window. As long as he had that pole, he thought, he and his dog would have plenty to eat. Finally, he climbed out into the cold night and, hanging from the window frame, lowered himself to the ground.

He slipped his pack onto his shoulders, picked up his fishing pole, and set out with his plan firmly in mind. He would go to the McClarens' house and get his puppy, and the two of them would hide out in the woods. They couldn't live in the woods forever, but he was sure they would be all right until he could figure out what to do next. It was not a good plan, of course. It meant leaving behind his mama and daddy, whom he loved very much, and finding a new place to live, which would be hard for a boy his age. But right now, Jeremy couldn't think about that. All he could think about was how much he missed his best friend. He knew that the quickest way to hike to the McClarens' farm was to follow the Creek for about two miles and then climb a steep hill. Careful to keep a good distance from the barn, he made his way to the creek and headed downstream.

The full moon had risen about an hour earlier, and all around, the snow seemed to glow in the soft light. Jeremy found that he didn't need his flashlight. That was good, because it left his right hand free to push branches out of his way while his left hand carried his fishing pole. Still, the cold wind and slippery ground made it hard to travel, and Jeremy's progress was very slow. After he had hiked about half a mile, he felt colder than he had ever felt in his life. His ears and hands hurt, and he couldn't even feel his nose.

"Boy, I can't wait to set up camp tonight," he said with trembling lips. "My sleeping bag will feel nice and warm, especially with Achilles in the bag with me."

Beneath a big oak tree, Jeremy stopped to rest for a while. He pulled the hood of his coat over his head, put his hands into his coat pockets, and pressed himself against the tree to escape the wind. After a few minutes, he felt a little better, and he set out again. About half a mile later, he came to Milford's Crossing. Here, the creek was about a hundred feet wide and, in most places, only a few inches deep, though in a few holes the depth reached a foot or more. To reach the McClarens' farm, he would have to cross the creek somewhere, and he knew that a little further downstream the creek grew narrower, but still too wide for him to jump across, and deeper. He decided that Milford's Crossing was the best place for him to cross.

Step by step, he picked his way across the creek, careful not to step into a hole that was too deep for his boots. Jeremy was good at walking in the woods, but he hadn't had much practice walking on snow or ice. So, when he stepped on an icy patch at the edge of the water, his foot slipped out from under him. He fell backwards, and his head struck a big rock just as his pack splashed into the water. Jeremy looked around, struggling to remember where he was and why. As he rolled over and rose to his knees, the trees seemed to dance, and the soft glow of the moonlight seemed as bright as the sun. A warm, wet feeling made its way down the back of his head and onto his neck. He touched his head and then saw that his fingers were red. His shoulders sagged, and he fell sideways into the cold, shallow water.

24

The wind carried a scent into the barn and to Thunder's nose. The scent woke Thunder from his sleep. It was a scent he knew well, but he was surprised to smell it. He lifted his head and sniffed the air. He stood and trotted out into the night, holding his nose high.

"Jeremy," he whispered. "And blood. Jeremy's blood!"

Jeremy was hurt, and even though he wasn't Thunder's human, Thunder still loved him and knew he had to help. He ran to the front door of the McClarens' house and began pawing at it and barking as fast and as loudly as he could. Soon the light above the door came on, the door opened, and Mr. McClaren stood in the doorway, yawning and rubbing his eyes.

"Sam, what is the matter with you?" he asked.

Thunder didn't understand what Mr. McClaren was saying, but he knew what he wanted to say to Mr. McClaren. Thunder wheeled around and darted toward the gate, looking over his shoulder. Mr. McClaren stayed in the doorway, so Thunder ran toward him and then turned and charged toward the gate again. Still, Mr. McClaren did not follow. Three more times, Thunder raced toward Mr. McClaren, spun around, and dashed toward the gate. Then he ran to the gate and began pawing at the latch, but Mr. McClaren did not move from the doorway.

"Settle down, Sam," Mr. McClaren groaned. "I have to get some sleep. Go lie down in the barn. I ain't opening that gate. You'll like this place fine once you get used to it."

Mr. McClaren turned off the light and went back to bed.

"What's wrong with Sam?" Mrs. McClaren asked as she rolled over and yawned.

"Seems to want me to let him out," Mr. McClaren answered. "Maybe he's homesick. Right smart dog. Sure wish he'd quiet down, though."

"He'll be all right," Mrs. McClaren sighed as she drifted back to sleep.

Outside, Thunder stood still as a statue, staring at the door. He didn't know what he should do. He wanted to follow the Father's plan, and he was sure that meant staying with the McClarens and taking care of them. Yet, Jeremy's scent still called to him, just as strongly as it had called to him the first time it reached his nose. As he stood in the yard, trying to figure out what to do, he suddenly saw a bright light, a light so bright that it made the snow look gray and dirty. Then he saw a man, a big man who seemed to be filled with light.

"Hello, old friend," said the shining messenger.

"Boy, am I glad to see you!" Thunder answered, almost shouting. "Do you have a message from the Father?"

"I do," answered the messenger.

"What should I do?" Thunder asked in a shaky voice.

"You must go to Jeremy, Thunder," said the messenger.

"How can I do that? I tried to get Lloyd to open the gate, but he wouldn't do it."

"You must go to Jeremy."

Then the light was gone, and, with it, the messenger. Thunder blinked as his eyes got used to the dimmer light. After a few seconds, the snow took on its former white glow, and Thunder began pacing like an angry bull. He ran to the gate and tried to lift the latch with his nose, but he found that a heavy padlock held the latch in place.

"What do I do?" he asked himself. "I have to go to Jeremy, but I'm stuck inside this fence."

As Thunder paced back and forth, faster and faster, his steps grew longer and his footprints deeper. He began to bounce and then to leap with every step. Suddenly, he realized, for the first time, what powerful legs the Father had given him. Pushing his feet against the ground as hard as he could, Thunder charged toward the fence, running faster than he had ever run in his life. With all his great strength, he leaped forward and upward. His front feet sailed over the fence, and, with one push against the top rail, his hind feet followed. Without stumbling, he hit the ground on the other side and bounded with giant strides toward the scent, toward Jeremy.

Soon, Thunder was across Mr. McClaren's field and into the woods. He never needed to turn from his course, for the scent on the wind told him exactly where Jeremy was, and Thunder was headed straight for him. After about a mile, he began to feel weary, but he refused to slow his pace. The cold, howling wind felt like tiny needles in his eyes, and thorns tore at his face and his ears. Flying over fallen trees and scrambling under low-hanging branches, he sped on toward

Jeremy. Finally, as he topped a small ridge, his eyes saw what his nose had already told him: his race was nearly finished. About twenty feet away, in the shallow water at the edge of the creek, lay Jeremy, still as an old log.

Seconds later, Thunder stood at Jeremy's side. He nudged Jeremy's head with his nose, but Jeremy did not move. He barked, whined, and pawed at Jeremy's shoulder, but Jeremy did not respond. Thunder licked Jeremy's face. He could smell and hear Jeremy's breathing, but Jeremy's skin was colder than it should be. Thunder's instinct told him to stay with Jeremy, keep him warm, and protect him. He knew he could do that, for the Father had given him a warm coat, big teeth, and powerful legs and jaws. He grasped the sturdy collar of Jeremy's coat in his teeth and dragged him out of the water onto the creek bank. He stretched his massive body over Jeremy and lay on top of him. Surely, in the morning, when the Dawsons discovered that Jeremy was gone, they would search for him. Until someone arrived, Thunder's body would keep Jeremy warm, and anything that wanted to hurt Jeremy would have to get past Thunder.

As Thunder waited, alert to every sound and smell, ready to fight any enemy, the white snow once again seemed to turn gray, and the shining messenger stood before Thunder.

"Thunder," he said.

"I did what you told me," Thunder answered. "I found Jeremy."

"Yes," said the messenger. "You have done well, but your work is not finished. Jeremy is hurt badly. He needs more help than you can give him, and he must have it very soon. You must stop a vehicle."

"The Father has made me very strong, and I can drag Jeremy easily," Thunder said. "If I move him to the side of the road, a vehicle will stop."

"No," answered the messenger. "This is very rough ground, with many rocks, fallen trees, and thorns. If you drag Jeremy, you will hurt him more. *You* must stop a vehicle."

Thunder's ears drooped. "But my mother taught me to stay away from moving vehicles. She said they were dangerous."

"Thunder, you *must* stop a vehicle."

Then the messenger was gone. Thunder's ears told him that the road was just a short distance away, up a small hill. He scampered up the hill and, just as he found the pavement, the lights of a car came into view. Thunder ran along the shoulder of the road toward the approaching car, barking and wagging his tail. As the car passed, he spun in his tracks and chased it, but soon the car had sped out of sight.

"I'll stop the next one," he shouted. He didn't have long to wait before a pick-up truck came rumbling along the road. This time, Thunder stepped into the truck's lane and charged toward it, barking wildly, ears pricked and eyes glowing in the headlights. As the truck swerved into the other lane, Thunder ran off the road and watched it pass, helpless to stop it. Thunder stood panting and hung his head. What good were his thick coat, his powerful legs and jaws, and his big teeth now? He remembered his mother's warnings about moving vehicles. He remembered the words of the shining messenger. Then he remembered something else his mother had told him: "If it was not too much for the Wounded One, it is not too much for us."

Thunder stepped into the road. "The next vehicle *will* stop," he said.

25

"**M**an, it's cold tonight!" Rich Blanding said, rubbing his hands together. "When are you going to get your heater fixed?"

"Heater? That's for wimps. We don't need heaters in these parts," Lance Jones laughed. "But you're right; it is mighty cold tonight. I need gloves just to handle this steering wheel. If I saw a fire right now, I don't think I'd want to put it out."

Rich and Lance were on their way to work the over-night shift at the Pondberry Fire Station.

"Well, if it's this cold tomorrow night," Rich complained, "I'm driving."

"Fine with me," Lance replied, "as long as your heater works."

Rich laughed. Then he leaned forward and squinted. "What's that up ahead?"

"Looks like . . . a dog," Lance answered, "and it's running right at us!"

"Hrrnk. Hrrrrrrrrrrrrrrrrrnk." The sound of Lance's horn filled the woods, but the dog did not stop or change direction. When the pick-up truck swerved, the dog swerved toward it.

"What in the world?" Rich shouted as the dog threw himself up onto the hood and crashed into the windshield. Screeching and sliding, the truck came to a stop on the shoulder of the road.

"You all right, Rich?" Lance asked.

"Yeah, you?"

"I'm fine," Lance answered, "but what in the world just happened? Did that dog just attack this truck?"

Lance opened the door.

"You sure that's a good idea?" Rich asked. "That was a big dog, and he looked crazy to me."

Lance pointed across the road to where the dog stood, with blood on his head, wagging his tail and holding one forepaw off the ground.

"Doesn't look so crazy now," Lance said. "Just looks hurt. I'm going to risk it. Come on, partner. Back me up."

The two men climbed out of the truck and approached the dog slowly. "Easy, boy," Lance said softly. "Nobody's going to hurt you. Just want to take a look at that leg."

Struggling to stay on his feet, Thunder watched as the two humans came toward him. As they approached, he backed away slowly, whining. Pain surged through his head and his left foreleg, and he felt the strength draining from his body, but he knew that he must not fall yet. Stopping the truck would be worth nothing if the humans didn't find Jeremy. He had to lead them to him. As Lance reached toward him, Thunder turned and started down the hill.

"Hang back, Rich," Lance almost whispered. "He may be less scared if there's only one of us."

Blood from the wound on Thunder's head ran down into his eyes, making it hard for him to see, but his nose still told him where Jeremy was. On three legs, he hobbled down the hill, twice stumbling and forcing himself to stand again. Finally, worn out, he felt his legs buckle beneath him, and he began to slide down the snowy hill. He came to a stop when his head struck a fallen tree. When he looked behind him, he saw Lance's hand a foot away.

"Not yet," he thought. "Not till I get to Jeremy. Just a little further."

Thunder bared his teeth and growled a growl that sounded as if it could melt the snow. Lance pulled his hand back and took a step backward. Thunder threw his head and his forepaws over the log and, yelping with pain as his injured leg rubbed against the ground, pushed his way over the log and under a low-hanging branch on the other side. He dragged himself a few more feet through the snow and laid his head on Jeremy's chest. Lance pushed past the branch and then stopped short when he saw Jeremy.

"Holy Mackerel!" he shouted. "Rich, we got a kid down here, and he's hurt bad! Looks like Evert Dawson's boy. Call it in and bring some blankets and the kit!"

As Lance's eyes moved back and forth between Thunder and Jeremy, his scent told Thunder that he was still a little afraid to approach. Forcing himself to his feet one last time, Thunder stumbled away from Jeremy and fell down in the snow. He watched as Rich came down the hill with blankets and a first-aid kid. Careful not to harm him further, the two men cut the straps on Jeremy's pack, bandaged his head, and covered him with blankets. Soon the wail of a siren made the pain in Thunder's head worse, and he watched the medics bring a stretcher. As Lance and Rich followed Jeremy and the medics back up the hill, Thunder's eyes closed.

Up the hill, on the road, Rich closed the door of the ambulance, and the big vehicle sped toward the hospital. As Rich and Lance watched the lights fade into the distance, they suddenly looked at each other. Both spoke at the same time.

"The dog!"

Lance spun around and headed back down the hill.

"He's probably a goner," came Rich's voice from behind him.

"He may be," answered Lance. "But after what he did, we've got to try. He's earned that much."

This time, Thunder lay still as the two men approached. Lance reached him first.

"Is he alive?" Rich asked.

"He's still breathing," Lance replied, "but just barely."

Carefully, Lance and Rich wrapped Thunder in Rich's thick, warm coat, carried him up the hill, and laid him in the back seat of the pick-up.

"I'll call Doc Mills on the way and ask him to meet us at the vet clinic," Rich said as the two men climbed into the front seat.

As the truck rattled down the road toward the vet clinic, a scent and a touch woke Thunder from his restless sleep. He had never smelled the scent or felt the touch before, yet neither one seemed new or strange. The scent was the scent of someone who was full of love and peace, someone who knew both great joy and great sorrow at the same time. The warm, soothing touch was the gentlest and the most powerful he had ever felt. As the loving fingers stroked his bloody head,

Thunder stretched and yawned, and his pain didn't seem quite so bad. Then Thunder heard a voice. It was calm and strong, and it seemed full of wisdom and power, as though it could never be disobeyed, and could never say anything that was not wise and true. The words the voice spoke filled Thunder with peace: "Good boy, Achilles. Good boy." Just before Achilles closed his eyes, he saw the hand that was touching him, and on the wrist, he noticed a scar.

26

Evert and Audrey Dawson sat in the hospital waiting room, trying to stay calm. Audrey sniffed, wiped her eyes, and sipped coffee. Evert bit his fingernails as he thumbed through the sports section of the newspaper. Both of them whispered prayers often.

"Dawson family?" a voice said.

"Yes, over here," Audrey answered, as she and Evert stood and started toward the doctor.

The doctor met them in the middle of the room. "Hi. I'm Dr. Brooks. Your son took a nasty blow to the head, he's lost some blood, and he got awfully cold out there. But I think he's going to be okay."

"Oh, thank you, Doctor, and thank the Good Lord," Audrey sobbed as she and Evert hugged each other.

"Yes, thank God," Evert sighed.

"We sewed up the cut on his head," Dr. Brooks continued, "and we've got him warmed up pretty well. I don't think the blood loss is bad enough that we need to give him blood. I'd like to keep him here for two or three days and then send him home. He'll need to take it easy for about three weeks, but after that he should be good as new. You should take him to see his regular doctor for a follow-up."

"Of course, Doctor. Whatever you say," Evert answered. "Thank you."

Dr. Brooks led the Dawsons into Jeremy's room. Jeremy was still sleeping, so his parents sat quietly. After a few minutes, a nurse appeared at the door.

"There's someone in the waiting room asking about Jeremy," she whispered. "Would you like to come talk to him?"

When Evert walked into the waiting room, he saw Mr. McClaren sitting on a sofa. Evert sat down next to him.

"Lloyd. Thanks for coming," Evert said. "Jeremy's had a rough night, but the doctor says he'll be fine."

Mr. McClaren squeezed Evert's shoulder with a strong hand. "Good to hear. Thank the Lord."

Evert cocked his head and wrinkled his brow. "How did you hear about it so soon?"

"Doc Mills saw my name on the collar when Lance and Rich took the dog in; he gave me a call. Told me the whole story—at least, as much of it as he knew. I figured I'd better come over here and check on my little buddy."

"Some story, isn't it? How's the dog?"

"Pretty banged up. Doc Mills says he's got a busted leg, a cut on his head, and some awful bad bruises. But he's still a puppy. He should heal pretty well. Doc says he'll need to take it easy for a while, but he should be okay in a month or two."

"Say, I'm really sorry, Lloyd. I can't figure out how Jeremy got that dog out of your yard with the padlock on the gate. I'll take care of the vet bills, and I'll make sure Jeremy knows that what happened doesn't change anything. Sam's still your dog."

Mr. McClaren raised his eyebrows. "*My* dog?" he asked. "Listen, Evert, I've been sitting here piecing things together. We had a good covering of snow on the ground at my house. I found dog tracks leading away from my fence, nowhere near the gate, but I didn't find any little boy tracks. That dog knew Jeremy needed help. He tried to get me to let him out, but I wouldn't do it. So he jumped a six-foot fence and went and found Jeremy. Then he near 'bout killed himself stopping Lance and Rich, and he led them to Jeremy. Sure, I could take that dog home, pen him up, maybe even keep him there. But he'll never be *my* dog. He's Jeremy's, and that's the Good Lord's doing. I've lived a long time, and I've seen a lot of things. But I ain't never seen nothing like what that dog did. If you're smart, you'll take an old man's advice and keep that dog."

"It just costs so much to feed him," Evert groaned.

"You'll manage," Mr. McClaren assured him.

"Well, Lloyd, I've known you for a long time, and you've never steered me wrong yet. Thank you. If Ginger ever has another litter of puppies, I'll see that you get one."

Mr. McClaren chuckled. "Well, I may take you up on that, but we'll talk about it when the time comes. You don't owe me a thing."

27

Two days later, the sun was shining and the air was chilly but not too cold when Evert and Audrey drove Jeremy home from the hospital. As they rolled to the edge of the yard on the old, dirt driveway, Jeremy saw Ginger come out from under the redtop hedge to greet them. He watched with wide eyes for a few seconds and then sighed. "No Achilles."

His mama patted his shoulder. "Cheer up, sweetie. You have a lot to be thankful for."

When the car came to a stop in the carport, Jeremy opened his door. Before he could climb out, his daddy scooped him up and carried him into the house.

"Aw, Daddy," Jeremy moaned. "I can walk."

"I know you can," his daddy answered. "But I don't get to carry you very often these days, and pretty soon you'll be too heavy, anyway."

Jeremy laughed. His daddy carried him into his bedroom and laid him gently on his bed.

"Now, the doctor says you need to take it easy," Evert said. "So you stay in your bed. Mama will stay here for a while and keep you company."

Evert kissed his boy on the forehead and left the room. Audrey sat down in a chair next to Jeremy's bed.

"Can I get you anything, honey?" she asked. "Would you like a glass of apple juice? How about a game of checkers?"

"No, thanks, Mama," Jeremy answered. "I just want to lie here for a while; I'm kinda tired. Maybe we can play checkers a little later."

"That sounds like a good idea. Okay if I just sit here for a little while?"

Jeremy settled into the bed and yawned. "That'll be good."

Out on the hard road, Achilles lay on a mattress in the bed of Mr. McClaren's pick-up. His left foreleg had a splint on it, and his ribs hurt when he breathed deeply, but his head felt much better, even with the stitches, and he could feel his strength coming back a little each day. When a familiar scent caught his attention, he raised his head to look over the side of the truck bed. In the distance, he saw the old, dirt driveway. He let out a tiny whine as he thought of Jeremy, and his head dropped back to the mattress. Then he noticed that the truck was slowing down and turning. When he raised his head again, he found that the truck was heading down the driveway toward the Dawsons' house.

"Yes! I remember now!" he whispered. "The Wounded One called me Achilles! That *must* be my true name! I *must* be Jeremy's dog!" He stood up and began to wiggle and bounce as best he could on three legs. After the truck stopped, Mr. McClaren climbed out of the cab and lowered the tailgate. Achilles was just about to jump out when Mr. McClaren caught him.

"Hold on, now. I don't think you're quite ready for that." Mr. McClaren lifted him out of the truck bed and set him gently on the ground. "Boy, you are a *big* dog," Mr. McClaren groaned as he straightened his back. The front door of the house opened, and Evert Dawson hurried to meet Mr. McClaren.

"Thank you, Lloyd. This is really nice of you, and it's going to make Jeremy feel a lot better. Now, what about the vet bills?"

Mr. McClaren winked and smiled. "That's all taken care of, and I don't want to hear another word about it."

Evert laughed and wiped his eye. "Well, after all this time, I know better than to argue with you." He grabbed Mr. McClaren and hugged him. "You're a real friend, Lloyd, a real friend. Thank you."

Inside the house, Jeremy stretched and yawned. His mama stroked his forehead.

"How are you feeling, Sweetie?" she asked.

"Not too good. Mostly tired."

"Well, I have a surprise that will make you feel a lot better. Look out the window."

When Jeremy lifted his head and looked, he nearly jumped out of bed. "Achilles!" he shouted. "Achilles! Mama! Is he . . . ? Can we . . . ?"

"Yes, Jeremy. He's your dog now. Take good care of him."

"I *will* Mama! Can he come inside? Please? Just for a while?"

Audrey sighed and laughed. "Well, I guess that'll be all right. Wait here."

Audrey went and opened the back door. "Okay, Jeremy," she called. "Call him!"

Out in the yard, when Mr. McClaren set Achilles on the ground, Ginger was there to greet him.

"It's good to see you, Thunder," she smiled.

Achilles held his head high, and his great chest swelled. "My name is Achilles, Mother."

"Then you have found your human."

"I have."

"Take good care of him, son."

"I will, Mother, or I'll give up my life trying."

From the back door came Jeremy's voice. "Achilles! Come on, boy!"

"I have to go, Mother," Achilles chuckled.

Ginger watched as Achilles hobbled around the corner of the house. A moment later, she heard Jeremy's voice again. "Good boy, Achilles! Good boy!"

Printed in the United States
By Bookmasters